Intersections

Jim Caldwell

Outskirts Press, Inc.
Denver, Colorado

This is a work of fiction. The events and characters described here are imaginary and are not intended to refer to specific places or living persons. The opinions expressed in this manuscript are solely the opinions of the author and do not represent the opinions or thoughts of the publisher. The author represents and warrants that s/he either owns or has the legal right to publish all material in this book.

Intersections
All Rights Reserved
Copyright © 2007 Jim Caldwell

Cover Image © 2007 Jim Caldwell
All Rights Reserved. Used With Permission.

This book may not be reproduced, transmitted, or stored in whole or in part by any means, including graphic, electronic, or mechanical without the express written consent of the publisher except in the case of brief quotations embodied in critical articles and reviews.

Outskirts Press
http://www.outskirtspress.com

ISBN-10: 1-59800-805-6
ISBN-13: 978-1-59800-805-0

Outskirts Press and the "OP" logo are trademarks belonging to
Outskirts Press, Inc.

Printed in the United States of America

to Jen, Chris and Allie... for your constant love and patience
to Beth ... for your expertise, caring and encouragement
to Kim ... for your support and affirmation
to Joanna and Terry ... for inspiring me to write
to the Capuchin Franciscans ... for a good education and
  a great *heritage*
to my friends ... for liking my stories whether you do or not
to anyone ... who strives to love and forgive

Dear Friend,

First of all thank you for buying my book and
supporting me. I really appreciate it..

Now, may I ask another favor? If you like
this novel, please help me out by going onto my web
site at Outskirts Press …..

www.outskirtspress.com/Intersections (capital "I" is important)

and clicking on both and
… and while on the respective sites:

1) **Click on "write a review" and compose a favorable sentence
   or two and,**

2) **Click on the "email a friend" hyperlink or "sent this page"
   (or whatever it says) to a friend, or two or ten. That is one or
   two or ten people that I do not know.**

Both actions raise my profile for "hits" to the sites and it
may generate more sales.

Thank you very much

Jim Caldwell

And I will teach you
that meeting is more than time and space

As our paths cross
I'll remind you of our need to treasure
the intersections

> Joe Wise, *Songprints.* Copyright © 1972
> by GIA Publications, Inc.
> Used with permission

One

It was not his ceiling. Even in his groggy stupor, Hunter intuitively knew that the ceiling he was staring at with one eye was not his room. He peered without moving. The other eye struggled to open, inhibited by morning, murky, mucous pasting the eyelid shut. It finally popped.

Hunter raised his head slightly. "Oh, my God!" Grabbing his forehead, he gently laid back down. A fast moving, thunderous train rolling forcefully down imaginary tracks on his brow could not have created as much of a pounding in his temples as what he was experiencing. "Ohhhh," he moaned, still grasping his brow in the full grip of his palm. The embattled line of thumping located itself directly behind the eyes. His nose was stuffed, adding to the bloated head. The taste in his mouth was excruciatingly sour. His whole body ached. In particular, his stomach felt like it had an insufferable desire to expel any and all contents. He again lay there motionless.

Somebody stirred across the room. Hunter turned slowly on the pillow. She budged again, face against the far wall in the other bed, groaning as she positioned herself in a ball and pulled the covers closer to her chin. Hunter unthinkingly knew it was Beverly. "Oh, my God. I'm in Alicia's bed." Without turning to look, he groped with his hand. His girlfriend was not beside him. Should he be dejected? Should he be sad? One thing was sure. He was confused. *Did I? Did we?* The throbbing, the dry mouth, and the unpleasant torso feelings diverted everything.

Alicia's roommate let out a burst of gas in her unconscious dream. Hunter winced. Disgusting bodily functions were never funny to him, notwithstanding his uncouth contemporaries.

And when did she come in?

With trepidation, the hand that had been comforting his head flipped the fluffy, flowered comforter and top sheet. Hunter raised himself ever so slowly and sat on the edge of the bed. The cool air chilled him. He was completely naked. Instinctively his hands shielded his privates as though the snoring female in the other bed would have had any chance of perceiving him in this anything-but-sexual state of appearance. He sat protecting himself nonetheless, squinting gingerly back and forth in a semi-circle. The atmosphere smelt of remnant incense burned only a couple of hours ago, but still lingering. Scented candles, each spent at different sizes in their own wax, dotted the room on the dressers, the desks and the bookshelves. Jewelry hung from the desk lamp nearest Hunter. It definitely was Alicia's dorm room, not his. The unresponsive body coiled under the covers was positively Alicia's roommate, not his. The fierce headache reared its ugly twinge again. He hunched over like the statue of the 'thinking man' trying to decide his next move.

Hunter's left tennis shoe lay sidewise near the door, obviously the first item to be shed in a hurry. The second was half way into the room next to his crumbled tee shirt and bundled jeans. A sweat sock was here, the second, there. He looked around for his underwear. The mustard colored shorts, with the phrase, *Hey, big boy*, repeated over and over, dangled on the front headboard. His boxers hung like a flag starved for a breeze. It signaled the last piece of apparel evidently discarded in a fit of passion. Hunter stretched in shear pain to retrieve them and warily slipped into them. He smirked though there was no humor in how he felt. He grimaced. He snickered while at the same time slightly shaking his bowed head. "Not the way I wanted it."

Beverly shifted again, this time completely facing him in a curled position, eyes shut as she wet her lips, grunted a little, and settled back into her sleep.

Hunter had to pee.

It was a shared bathroom. Despite what might have happened hours before, Hunter locked the door to the other room out of natural modesty as he lifted the seat. The smell of hair sprays and sundry items punctuated the air. As he relieved himself, he thoughtlessly put the cap on the opened toothpaste lying on the back of the toilet next to the box of feminine hygiene products. Just bending forward accentuated the throbbing in his head.

Flow from the sink faucets in institutions takes forever to warm up. Hunter splashed the bleak cold water on his face and relieved the ache somewhat. He inventoried the products sitting out as well as the ones cramming the half opened cabinet on the wall. The mirror, although slanted, was not very friendly. Grabbing one, a tiny travel bottle, Hunter swigged, swished, spit and rinsed. An actual idea occurred. Rummaging around again but finding only prescriptions, pills to relieve monthly periods, he heaved a sigh. There was nothing visible for a headache.

"Crap."

The cruel late summer sun streaming in the only window made matters worse. It inundated the chaotic space with light, illuminating a calamitous dorm room in the all female residence. Alicia and Beverly's place featured posters of shirtless, masculine-looking celebrities papering the walls as opposed to the barely clad feminine counterparts decorating Hunter and Brian's room across the quad. But the rest was common to both: clothes hanging off the back of chairs and on open closet doors, empty, stained coffee cups and used fast food containers sitting on top of dust laded stereo speakers, books laying half opened, stacked upon each other, as though waiting for the continuation of honest study moments.

Hunter caught a glimpse of the 5" x 7" portrait of Alicia's parents peeking out from the far left corner of the cluttered desk. She introduced them as they moved in for the new semester. He liked them. The thought of what might have transpired the night before reoccurred. *Oh, my God.* Hunter closed his eyes as though everything would go away, and when he opened them he would be in his 10:00 creative writing class.

"Shit! What time is it?" He looked for his watch. It was gone from his wrist. Was he late? *Did I sleep in?* He shoved knickknacks of tiny bears scattered around on the small shelf above the bed. Not there. He shuffled papers and books on the desk. Not there, neither. With both hands on the top of his head, he saw it. "Crap!" Hunter blurted aloud then covered his mouth to quiet himself. It wasn't necessary to wake Beverly and add to his woes. The watch was on his arm all the time, pushed up almost to the elbow. *God, what a morning.* And it was only 9:12 a.m.

The fire drill was on: pants and shirt donned almost concurrently, socks and shoes recovered. Hunter sat on the floor tying the second lace. His wallet, his room key, he searched again. They had remained intact in their respective pockets during the unceremonious undressing. In with his key was the coaster, the souvenir. It caused him to smile. He stood there holding it.

It wasn't as though Hunter had never been there before, but last night was special. When he turned 21 early last April, he and Alicia were just acquaintances. With the new

Intersections

semester and the flourishing friendship between them, she had arranged a surprise 21st and a half birthday bash 'just for fits an' kicks'. Any excuse for a good time.

Everyone at the three tables signed it. The plethora of names just about obscured the name of the bar and the sexy, bikini-dressed woman holding the cocktail glass in the logo. Alicia had started it, writing 'Happy Half Birthday, my love' on the very top with the date.

Hunter ran his finger down Alicia's class schedule taped on the base of the desk lamp. *Biology at ten ... Hartley Hall.* The head was getting better with activity, but not by much. He would struggle.

Within minutes of reaching the end of the second floor of Phiny Hall Hunter needed to return. Coeds living in the same dorm eyed him up and down and giggled as he tucked in his shirt. The wooden floorboards of the oldest building at Garrison U. creaked as he ran back to Alicia's room. It was one of the first edifices on the campus, renamed in 1950 for a highly successful alumnus, one of the first woman CEO's in the city, who richly donated every year until her death. The building unquestionably needed attention.

Right hand on his chest near his neck, Hunter searched again with an even more intent fervor than the hunt for the watch. It wasn't on the desk unless it was buried beneath one of the many piles of stuff. He moved a few items but with no luck.

What did I do with it?

In desperation, Hunter pulled drawers open on either side and closed them. The bookshelf right above didn't have it. He rifled the chains hanging on the lamp. He examined the floor around Alicia's chair on his hands and knees. He inspected the open space in the middle, what little there was. Feeling under the bed as far as he could reach for the missing object caused the temple pounding to resume.

"Dammit!"

Beverly didn't hear a thing.

Jim Caldwell

All he found was a candy paper and a ripped condom wrapper. "Ohhhh!" He moved the tiny bears again figuring that was the most logical place to throw it.

"Oh my God, I tossed it! Must have. It's gone! Where the hell is it?"

Standing there dumfounded, Hunter tapped his jean pockets. Frustrated, he slammed his hand on the bed.

"Shit!"

He didn't care this time if he disturbed Beverly. He did. She startled, opened her eyes, and then concluded it wasn't worth fully awakening.

Hunter threw the cover and top sheet on the floor. It wasn't there. He patted the bottom sheet as though tactile investigation would reveal something that sight did not. The sensual smell of bodies from the night's repose still lingered. The questions of *'Did we?'* shot through his brain once more.

The college senior had 22 minutes to get his notebook and text from his own dorm and be on time for class. Professor Chariton was a stickler for punctuality, or *"don't come at all"*, he would declare.

"Dammit!"

Hunter left the room a second time, without the chain. *Oh, I hope she did something with it.*

"And like it's the same shade as my old high school sweater a couple of years ago."

"I hate sweaters," her classmate in the gray hooded mackinaw chimed, "never did. Too confining, if you know what I mean."

"Girls, girls," the third companion said, "the hell with this nonsense. Anyone get Henderson's quiz finished? I need the last few answers." She cooed and rocked. "I was *very* busy last night, and didn't get done." Everyone laughed.

"So I take it that the half birthday was *celebrated*," the person who initiated the sweater talk said, *"completely?"*

Intersections

Alicia pulled her face close to her chest, books up to her mouth. "I'll never tell." The threesome laughed again. "Now, girls, please. What are the differences between plant and animal eukaryotic cells?" She held her biology textbook flat, the page lying on top as she prepared to write.

Marcy opened her own backpack at her feet to accommodate her. "The main differences between plant and animal eukaryotic cells are that plant cells contain cell walls, —"

Alicia stopped writing, completely preoccupied with Hunter coming up behind her friends. She could see he was disheveled and upset. "Well, goooood morning, party boy. What's a matter? A little headache?" Her companions turned and giggled.

"Can we talk?" Hunter steered her apart from the group. He whispered to her with his back to the other coeds. "Ummm, ummm. What happened last night?" He shuffled his feet and his whole body. "Did we?"

Alicia was coy. "You don't remember?" She slid her hand down his cheek. "Lover boy, I'm so surprised at you."

How could she sound so seductive this early in the morning? Hunter was not amused. "Come on, Alicia. Did anything happen?"

"Come on, yourself."

"But you know I wanted it to be special."
She batted her eyes. "And how do you know it wasn't?"

Alicia was being so capricious and playful that Hunter couldn't separate truth from fiction, especially with a hangover. The classmates were eavesdropping. His headache warranted against clear thinking.

I'm perturbed to say the least, he almost blurted out loud.

And maybe this wasn't the time or place. But Hunter was anxious to know. He held on to her arm. "Please."

Alicia broke away, unrelenting in the game. "Wellll ... when we left the crowd last night, you were soooo lovelydovely and clinging to me ... soooo..."

"Come on, Alicia, we're late. Let's go." The two waiting coeds danced. "Come on or we're goin' without you!"

Waving her hand in a whimsical way, Alicia yelled back, "Call me... this afternoon ... after your technical theatre."

Together the juniors scurried away, down along the column of evergreens lining the walk towards the biology building. He watched as Alicia dropped her papers and stooped to gather them and continue running. The quad bristled with students and a few professors. Someone bumped Hunter. "Oh, sorry, man." He stood there, unsatisfied.

"Today we will begin exploring the plays of August Wilson, who was the cofounder with Rob Penny, scriptwriter, and director of *Black Horizons on the Hill*. We will begin with *Turner's Come and Gone* for which he won the Antoinette Perry Award nomination for best play this year" Professor Chariton pointed. "Mr. Harrisson, would you please begin our dramatic reading, paying close attention to the vocal directions."

Hunter did not respond.

"Mr. Harrisson?"

"What? Oh, I'm sorry." Unshaven, bleary and hurting, Hunter stammered in embarrassment.

The literary arts professor aggravated the situation. "Too much partying last night, Mr. Harrisson? I noticed that you barely made it this morning." The class of 17 laughed. "Well, let's move over to Miss Gearly." The stocky, brunette student three desks to Hunter's right started to read.

"Missed you last night after the blowout, bro. Guess you *finally* got some." Brian smacked his roommate on the back shoulder. "Of course what am I saying?" He slapped himself up the side of the head. "I was so drunk myself I didn't know you weren't in the room until this morning."

Intersections

Hunter fumbled for the correct change in front of the vending machines just inside the student union. "You *do* remember that I beat you at pool, *don't you*?" The answer was of utmost importance to Brian as evidenced in his inflection. "Man, you were sooooo wasted. And, I must say, right now you sure don't look good. In fact, you look like shit, man!"

Thanks for the compliment

Brian punched the coffee machine. "Too bad, they don't have one of these filled with the dog that bit you." Hunter did not laugh.

The java was bitter and not that hot. He scrunched his face. There was no appetite for any food at all. Almost revulsion.

Tacked upside down to the corkboard on the door to his room was a pink, scented note: "Hey, meet me later... at the union ... love ya.... A."

The hell with it!

Hunter headed to his bed. He would blow off the afternoon classes.

Two

The brightly dressed, middle-aged woman rested her chin on her closed fist, looking out the large glass panorama at the small whitecaps crashing on the break wall. Winds were kicking up on Lake Erie, a sign of the forecasted cold front. Birds landed more on the shore than on the rocks. In the distance, way beyond the two visible fishing boats, where the sky kisses the water, a demarcation line approached. Perhaps it was an allegory. This morning had been beautiful, but rain was coming. Julie Harrisson hoped that the temperatures would not change too drastically as she had worn a light jacket to her lunch date.

She shifted to having both elbows on the table, her hands folded, almost in prayer, touching her lips and nose. Waiting quietly, Julie tilted her head slightly, the few strands of gray streaking her long, brown hair reflecting the light bouncing in the window. A candle centerpiece on the table of this quaint Inn cast a serene look on her small, oblong face. Any professional photographer would have choreographed this; or an artist would have posed her this way as part of a portrait. But a closer look, with more light, would reveal lines of stress and struggle etched in Julie's countenance over the past years.

I wonder what she looks like? Wonder how much she's changed over time?

She felt nervous in her anticipation. The space between her palms filled with her warm breath. The closeness of her hands to her lips caused Julie to fog the lower portion of her small-rimmed eyeglasses. She retrieved a Kleenex from her purse to clean them.

Mild conversations surrounded her. Talk among friends, the sharing of problems and current events, perhaps like her and Elena, a reunion. But Julie was oblivious to it all, caught up in memories and the beauty of the lake she loved so much. It was one of the reasons she and Russell had moved into Mentor when they married. Neither was originally from the region.

"Can I get you something to drink, Mrs. Harrisson," the petite young waitress asked, breaking into her meditation, "while you're waiting?"

Julie moved her hands from her mouth. "Well, hi, Darlene. I didn't know you worked here."

"I just started Wednesday. I'm supposed to work on the weekends and one night a week," she answered and then rattled her head from side to side. "But that's going to change. My Dad doesn't like me working on school nights."

"I understand. I don't like that either for the twins." Darlene was a regular at their house, a friend of one of Julie's daughters. Both were juniors at Mentor High School.

"Could I have a hot tea?"

She recalled one of the traditions of the Inn. "Is this one of the days I can get English tea?"

"No. That's Tuesdays and Thursdays. Not on the weekend."

"Oh, okay." Julie put her hands on her lap. "You know

Jim Caldwell

the lady I'm waiting for is from England." She nodded towards the empty chair opposite her. "She's a doctor in London."

"Really?"

"We haven't seen each other for a little over 20 years."

"Wow." Darlene put her pad and pencil back into the large embroidered pocket on the front of the Victorian uniform. The dress fit the ambiance of the Inn. "I'll be right back with your tea."

More patrons began to fill the dining room. As the sky darkened, the candles took prominence. Classical music permeated the room at just the right volume and tempo. What a peaceful place it was for two former classmates to rendezvous.

Aston Inn was originally the main house of a vast grape farm in the last century. The Victorian Italianate home from the 1800's was listed on the National Register. When the Butero family purchased it in 1960, they converted it to a bed and breakfast. The dining room was widened and expanded to provide a fine restaurant for the guests as well as the local vicinity. It's location a few miles from town offered a relaxing repast for those visiting the antique malls and wineries nearby. The people of Mentor cherished Aston as a great community treasure. It was *the* perfect place to invite Elena.

Wonder if she still laughs that silly little girlish way?

Julie wet her lips. She recalled something she forgot to do. Opening a tiny black appointment book, she made a note for 9:30 the coming Tuesday morning.

A few little crafts nearby, still waiting to be dry-docked and stored for the winter, bobbed up and down with the growing wind. Digging deeper into the purse Julie squeezed on some peach hand cream, lost in the thought of two young women anxious to become nurses and "save the world" some 25 years ago.

Wonder if she ever married?

Intersections

Massaging her hands was relaxing.

Julie sipped her tea and returned to the lake. Elena Meltrant was late. That was not unusual. She was the only one in their class that Julie ever remember being late even for tests because she was still cramming in the hall to get a perfect grade. No one was surprised when she was named valedictorian with a perfect 4.0.

"Julie." The maitre d' led her to the table.

Julie turned quickly to see the tall, distinguished woman before her. "Elena." The two embraced warmly, and stood there holding both hands, visibly filling the years in one minute. "Wow, just as I thought. I aged and you didn't."

"Oh, you're so full of it." It was the Elena she knew. "Thank you so much for the invitation. But how did you know I would be in town?"

"I saw the story in the newspaper that you were speaking."

"Makes sense. It is so good to see you. But then how did you get my number?"

"I called the medical society and explained that we were classmates in nursing school before you went on to higher things. They were reluctant at first, but I convinced them I was sincere."

"I must admit your call was the most pleasant surprise of all."

There was not even a hint of sun left out the window. An overcast sky clouded the scene but not the beauty. Stray fishermen left the pier. The guests visiting the gift shop next door, which was originally the smoke house, scurried back the path to the main house a little more wind blown.

"You look great, Julie." The two had settled across the table from each other. "And I love that blouse. You always did dress well."

"Thank you." She smiled broadly, "Doctor."

Elena Meltrant reacted. "Oh, titles, titles. Oh, how we like titles."

"But you've earned it." Julie reached and squeezed her hand.

"I suppose."

"Are you staying at the same hotel?"

"As the conference? Yes. Downtown Cleveland. I forget the name." Elena did that funny little chuckle. "It starts tomorrow, for three days. I talk tomorrow night." She raised her hand to her nose. "Mmmm, that cream you have on smells great." It was the same Elena, all right, simply down to earth despite being a reproductive endocrinologist for London's prestigious Picadilly Hospital. As a fertility specialist, she had written extensively about endometriosis and fibroid surgery. She was published. She was world renown.

Elena carried herself in a stately manner, her hair completely silver, and her face tender for the needs of couples wishing to conceive. She, too, dressed well. British by birth, she spoke with a delightful accent, which their classmates adored. Maybe that was the initial characteristic that endeared her to everyone. But it was her passion for caring that her roommate remembered most. "Tell me about yourself, Julie. Your family. Catch me up on these many years." She laughed again 'that silly little girlish way'. It was the only trait that seemed out of character.

"Well, Russell and I had an anniversary a little more than a month and a half ago. In fact," she pointed in the air, "we spent it here." There was an odd twist to Julie's tone and body language that caught Elena's attention.

"Any other kids besides–?" She fought for a name, "Hunter?"

"Yes, that's right. I always loved that name you picked."

"Yeah. We have a set of twins. Seventeen-year-old girls, Lynn and Lonnie. They're both juniors at Mentor High School ... and typical teenage girls with the boys and all. But they're also quite different, one is very sports minded while Lynn is more like her brother, more partial to the arts."

"Is he in college?"

"Up in New York, at Garrison University. It's a small liberal arts school he picked because of their theater arts program. He's hoping to be on stage in New York City someday."

"Fantastic.

"Turned 21 this year."

"Wow. Yeah, that's right, it's about that long. Gee, time flies when you're having fun."

Julie wanted a dialogue. "And you ... do you have any children?"

A sorrowful look overcame Elena. "No...no kids." She spoke lower. "Ironic, isn't it ... that I spend my days helping other couples have a baby."

"You're married?

Elena sat back. "Oh, I've always used my maiden name for my profession." She juggled her hands to help explain. "It's ... well you get established writing and lecturing ... and I guess it's like having a stage name." Lifting her napkin, she wiped a drop of her own tea from the corners of her lips. "But that can be a problem ... as I found out." She laid the linen back on the table.

"Yes, I was married. Twelve years. But you know what they say. Two career professionals will eventually get in each other's road ... the competing for attention ... well, let's just say that it strangles the giving necessary in an honest relationship."

Julie had her chin on her knuckles again, studying intensely the woman across from her. Understood, she did, and reacted accordingly with a motion of the head.

"And definitely prevents starting your own family. Two doctors giving 20 hours a day to study and practice leaves little time to nurture," she hesitated, "or heal a marriage. Ironic."

Silence.

It was unique that Elena could be so personal as though

they had spoken only the week before instead of years ago. Julie envied her openness. "My career left little time for kids of our own ... or for that matter, time for the two of us." Finishing her tea, Elena stared out at the lake, then turned back to Julie. "Oh, well... Tell me more about you and your family. What does your husband do?"

"Attorney."

"Good."

"In Cleveland, not too far from the hotel where you're staying. He's in with three others. Been there the last five and a half years." Julie paused. The slightly distressed tone came back into her voice. "He originally started by himself, right here in Mentor, but was offered a deal to join a larger practice. It's been quite a change for us." The last words were spoken as though it were an explanation of something.

Julie redirected the conversation. "Hey, any chance you can stay a few days after the convention? Spend Thanksgiving with us?"

"I don't know. I didn't really plan on staying." She knew full well there was no one waiting for her return.

"Come on, Elena. You're welcome to stay as long as you can. I'd be honored. I'd love to have you meet the girls. And Hunter will be home for the holiday. You'll get to see him again. But he's a little bigger. No, I take that back. He's a *lot* bigger since the last time you saw him." The women laughed. Elena noticed the non-mention of Russell.

"Yeah, I think I would like that." This time Elena reached for Julie's hand. "Yeah, I think I will. Thank you for asking."

"Tell you what," Julie followed, "turn your rental car in at the hotel and let me know when to pick you up."

"I'm not sure what time the final banquet will be over. I'll knock you up when we're finished."

Julie burst out with laughter and promptly covered her mouth. It had been too long since she heard the British idiom for 'calling on the telephone'. "Sorry."

Intersections

There was pinging on the window. The rain had started blowing droplets of rain a number at a time in a steady rhythm on the pane. The lake was churning. Elena commented on its beauty. Together they shared memories for two hours, reliving funny episodes at Drexel University and the College of Nursing and Health Professions. They recalled professors and fellow students.

"Do you ever see Debbie Kerly?"

"Three, four years ago. Ran into to her while we were on vacation in Myrtle Beach. She was on her second marriage with a total of five kids between the two relationships. Hunter actually flirted with her daughter who was his age at the time." Elena raised an eyebrow in conjunction with a grin. "Wouldn't that have been funny, my son and my arch rival's daughter?" Julie shuttered, "oh, just the thought of it." The two laughed again and again.

There were stories about other classmates and where they might be today. They spoke of parents and people they knew in common and wondered about them. They shared their volunteer days in the war and how naïve they were about real life combat and the ugliness of the battlefield. Recalling how they went their separate ways for family and careers, both regretted that the rush of routine life robbed them of staying in touch.

"Did you ever run into anyone we worked with in Da Nang?" Elena put one hand over top the other in front of her on the table as Darlene cleared the empty plates. Julie knew what was behind the question.

"No. But if you remember I wasn't deployed there as long as you." Julie looked to the lake to assuage past memories and turned back. "Right before I found out I asked to be transferred to Reinstat, Germany. Hunter was born there on the base."

"Yeah, now I recall. Do you know where he's living today?"

"No. I've never tried to look him up. I knew it couldn't

work and his life was in so much turmoil at the time. I just thought it was best for both of us that I move on." Julie shrugged, her hands resting upright on her lap. Elena saw the tension in her face. She surmised that it wasn't because of what happened years ago. "And Russell became a great support. We met each other in Germany."

"You mean he's never known?"

"No."

"Well, does your son know?

"No."

Silence again.

Elena had uncovered one of the causes of the stress lines. Benevolently, she laid her hand on top of Julie's hand as it rested near her wrinkled napkin. "Don't you think it's time?"

"I suppose," Julie answered with very little enthusiasm.

She swiftly switched the topic. "Hey, guess what? There's a TV show that just started here in the states that takes place in My Khe. Some of the nurses in it remind me of our whole crew."

"Really? China Beach?"

"Yeah, good old China Beach. In fact, that's the name of the show. Started last April and is kind of popular. I've watched it a number of times."

"Interesting."

It touched off another round of shared memories, this time about the place where they nursed wounded soldiers back to health both with their skilled talents as well as pleasant personalities.

The pungent smell of mushrooms wafting from the sizzling steak as a waiter swished passed their table triggered something very disturbing. Julie's stomach reacted. She abruptly rose from the table.

"Excuse me."

Would she make it to the ladies room in time without being embarrassed?

Intersections

She sat on the seat, calming her body with long deep breaths. It wasn't happening. Female patrons fixed their hair and their make-up and adjusted themselves at the mirrors. The stall doors on either side opened and closed. Julie was about to be humiliated. With urgency and loud noises, she threw up her lunch and a lot more.

Three

The word is *believed* to be a corruption of 'bone fire' deriving from a Celtic midsummer festival where animal bones were burnt to ward off evil spirits." Casey Rankos jumped in front of Hunter and the others, legs spread eagle and hands in the air like he was a guard on a basketball team. His tone was the mocking, pedantic manner he often used. His friends knew him as the trivia intellectual in their crowd, forever regaling everyone with the meaning of everything, from life to the spectacular light the collegians approached.

Tanya Nickols, the committee chairperson had done a fantastic job directing the logs to be piled in a massive teepee-looking structure. Flames stretched high into the night as though they were striving to cinch the puffy low-lying clouds of late October. A darkened sky, just a day or so from the last quarter moon, gave way to a vast flickering light over the far end of Shanny field by the home goal post. It would be a fun night to let out all the stress of mid-term week by screaming and rallying for a team that at best had a 50-50 season. Tonight was the last game of the season and although there was no hope of playoffs, it was 'senior night', a special time to give the graduating football players their recognition.

Hunter did not play. His talent was speaking and acting. Coach Walstor asked him to present the seniors and charge up the crowd. He sought out Tanya near the stacked bales of hay to the left of the fire. "Everything okay?"

"Hunter, thank God you're here. We can't get the damn microphones to work." Feedback pierced the air, even cutting into the noise of students streaming in from every direction as well as filling the bleachers. People grasped their ears.

"Ahhaaa!"

"See what I mean. Help!" She threw her hands up in frustration.

Hunter knew the portable soundboard from the University Theater well. He had run it a million times, outdoor concerts, commencements, karaoke night at the coffee house. A few turns of knobs, a few switching of plugs and the problem was solved.

"You're the greatest! Thanks." Tanya hugged him. Hunter lifted her off the ground with a return hug. "By the way, Walstor wants to run out with the team in dramatic fashion. Can you start us off in about 10 minutes? I'll go give them a countdown."

"Yep."

Brian attacked Hunter jumping horseback on him, almost toppling him to the ground. "Hey, bro. You and Alicia going to the 'Ratz' after the game?"

"Don't know. Haven't been able to get Alicia." Hunter searched the crowd for a sign of his girlfriend. "We've been missing each other the past couple of days."

She was climbing the benches with Marcy and her gang heading to the very top. Grabbing the mike, Hunter barked in a deep, baritone, announcer-like voice. "Attention. Attention. Testing. One, two, three. One, two, three..." He followed with the proverbial tapping on the microphone. "Would Miss Alicia Collier please make yourself visible to be recognized by the crowd?" People looked around, laughing, trying to spot the supposed 'celebrity'.

Alicia too burst out laughing, waving and jumping. "Here I am! Here I am! Up in peanut heaven!"

"And at right guard, weighting 240, Charlie 'Tractor-pull' Robe..." Hunter, teetering on the stacked bales of hay, almost fell. He closed his eyes hard and opened. With blurred vision, he had suddenly gotten dizzy.

Maybe the flickering of the massive flames?

It broke his concentration. Jumping, boisterous revelers hesitated at the interruption. Hunter made a joke and continued, looking up to Alicia in the far distance. She wasn't with her friends. "At left guard, weighting ..."

Scott Pincolior thrust his face past Alicia's and kissed her neck. The pair stood near the back on the side of the bleachers. Shoving her underneath, the six-foot senior displayed his aggressiveness. "Any chance, Beverly can disappear again tonight?"

His lips remained at her right ear. "Wherever she goes when—" He nibbled her ear lobe.

"Ah, Scott, I don't think so." Fighting the feelings in her body, Alicia spoke with her heart. "I think I just don't want this anymore."

"But you and I make such passionate music together." He was panting on her neck without eye contact. "Like wild tango stuff." Slowly and sensually he drew out the 'tango' word. "Or is that just grunts I hear?" His laugh was cynical.

Alicia pushed him off her, trying to walk around him. "No, I'm serious Scott. And besides, I promised Hunter I'd hang out with him and his friends at the 'Ratz'."

" Oh, the wimpy, theater-boy."

Alicia was incensed. "Dammit, you're so full of yourself. You don't know a damn thing about him and I *resent* your stupid put downs." She tried to get past and leave.

"Whoa. Looks like someone's falling." Scott stroked her cheek. She pulled away. "Does he know that you and I sleep together?" He sneered, "as recently as a few weeks ago?"

Alicia turned her face sideways. "No. And I never want him to." She confronted him with piercing eyes. "It's just sex with you, Scott. And I don't want it anymore." Her voice softened. "It's so different with Hunter. He cares... about me ... about someone else beside himself." She no longer looked at him but past him.

"But we're just having fun ... *Dee-Alici-ous.*" The sarcastic pet name disgusted her. It seemed sultry that night last year when she lost her virginity to him, the play on words with her name and the adjective, delicious. But now she resented it. Scott reached to stroke again. "And you know you want it as much as I do. It doesn't have to interfere with you and", he dripped with sarcasm, "theater-boy."

Inside, Alicia battled to resist her strong physical attraction for Scott. Good things were happening between her and Hunter the past few weeks. She desired that more but didn't know how to cleanly break from her mistaken past. Her head was down. "Ah, maybe Sunday. Bev's going home for a dentist appointment early Monday morning." Alicia regretted what she just said, but mumbled it anyhow. Helpless to combat what her heart told her was all wrong for her, she hated herself at that moment. Was she scared of him and what he might reveal, or simply addicted to a bad relationship?

"That's better." Scott swaggered out from the beams supporting the bleachers, allowing her free passage. "I don't have to tell. *But someone else might if--*" The contemptuous threat was meant just how it sounded. It stabbed Alicia's gut.

Jim Caldwell

Hunter had the crowd in his hand. A born entertainer, he was at home on any stage. He couldn't wait to tell Alicia that he had landed the part of Leon Tolchinsky in Neil Simon's *Fools* at Rawly Theater at the end of January. Maybe she would join the set crew. That way they would be together for all of the rehearsals.

"Do we have the best damn school or what? And what about these seniors! Come on, guys, let's give it up for the Class of '88!" He jumped; he swung the mike by the cord, and signaled for the music to be turned up full tilt. The crowd roared. They were electrified by the heavy bass rhythms. It caused every foot in the stadium to be dancing.

Dizzy again, Hunter licked his dry lips.

Maybe I just need something to eat.

Scott strutted back, blocking Alicia again from returning to her friends. He slid his hand down the side of her light brown hair and leaned in to smell it as he had often done. Then reaching to the back of her head, Scott pulled her lips to his for a long, tongue-plunging, passionate kiss. At first she staunchly resisted, but as her body melted, Alicia went with it, feeling a gut wrenching guilt. "Can't resist me, can you... *Dee-Alici-ous*! Wait till Sunday. I'll make you feel soooo good." He let go. "You are so gorgeous. I will go nuts until then." Alicia managed a scrunch between a smile and a frown. She climbed towards her friends, a wretched pit in her stomach.

The stadium went wild. Hunter had them at a frenzied pitch. Football players circled the fire, clenched fists in the air. On cue, the bales that created the temporary stage were tossed into the flames. Sparks shot everywhere. Part of Tanya's crew tossed small firecrackers for finale effect. The students loved it, screaming and yelling. Tanya herself was clapping furiously. "Yeah! Yeah!" The rally was a grand success. More than one charged up player as well as coeds hugged Hunter. Adrenaline flowed plentifully. Wishing Alicia were down on the field next to him, he stumbled from being jostled and squeezed ... and dizzy.

"You are the greatest." Marcy hugged Hunter as he reached them half way down the bleacher steps. "You should get a job as a circus barker. You could make millions." Hunter didn't know whether that was a compliment or a put down. It didn't matter. He saw only Alicia.

"Hey." He said, wrapping his arms fully around her.

"Hey."

"Going to the 'Ratz'?"

"I think so." No usual bantering: "I don't know. Maybe. Why, do you know someone that's going that I might know?" Alicia was not her bubbly self.

Crowded wasn't the proper description of the *Gin and Rummy Ratz Keller.* It was wall to wall with collegians, swapping barbs and beers and horror stories of what might have happened during mid terms. Honest discussion was destroyed in favor of pandemonium and sheer silliness. It was a night to blow off steam, and nobody would deny them.

Hunter and Alicia wedged between groups, drinks held high to get to their friends' long, confiscated table away from the bar. Hunter loved being thrust up against her body out of protection from the masses. Something was happening taking their relationship to a deeper level. Hunter could not be distracted by the noise from his feelings and sense of wonderment. He defended her from deliberate jabs of those trying to take advantage of the crowded party atmosphere to cop a feel. He shielded and safeguarded her from unintended, protruding elbows and groping hands.

Does she know how much I really love her?

"I missed you the past couple of days."

"What?" Alicia yelled across the table. It was a lost cause. They could do no more than act as silly as the whole room. She tossed a peanut from the bowl at him. It bounced off his forehead.

Hunter responded with his own throw, only to have her catch it in her open mouth. The group laughed and clapped.

Does she feel the same way about me that I feel about her?

This time of the year in mid-state New York should be colder. Everyone said this year was unusually warm, and nobody was complaining. Hunter's previous years had snow and ice as early as this. Garrison was 70 miles northwest of Rochester, north of Buffalo where winter comes early and stays late in the infamous Snow Belt off Lake Erie. But tonight Alicia and he wore only light coats, the same ones they had on at the rally.

It was 3:00 a.m., and still no wind or cold temperatures to chill them. The quad was deserted with half of the crowd still whooping it up at the 'Ratz' and the other half, that partied too fast and too furious, passed out in theirs or someone else's room. Walking in a playful mood, fingers entwined, the couple swung their arms in unison. "Oh, that was fun tonight."

Hunter stopped abruptly. "Let's sit." He was dizzy again and very thirsty.

What the hell's the matter with me?

Together they reached one of the metal-pounded benches along the way, strategically placed to add to the stately academic look of the corridor running the length of the campus.

"You okay?"

"Yeah. I must have a touch of something. I got dizzy a couple of times today." What he did not say was that it had happened before today, often.

Alicia rested her head against his chest, laying her hand near his heart.

Hunter surrounded her with his arms. "Tired?"

"A little. But it's so nice out here. Let's stay a little more." Alicia looked up into his hazel eyes, a number of shades lighter than his hair. She noticed that he needed a haircut as he usually wore his hair cropped closer. Tonight it fell down his forehead in a free-for-all. Reaching, Alicia ran her fingers through it up to the top of his scalp. Sliding down his cheek, she pressed into the dimple she loved so much. He smiled at the soft touch of her hand.

"Sure." Hunter felt peaceful and right to be holding her.

She felt the same.

I could stay here forever.

They allowed each other to be quiet.

Tracing the object around his neck under his shirt, she asked,

"Did you get a new one?"

"New chain?"

"Yeah."

"Yeah, I broke the other one in two places when I tossed it ... *that night.*" He sounded embarrassed at the last two words. "Sorry, again for getting so smashed-faced that night. That's not really me." He kissed her on the forehead.

Still touching his shirt, Alicia sketched the outline of the piece of jewelry underneath with her thumb. "You were so upset until we found it. Why is this cross so special to you?"

"Oh, long story."

"We've got time. It's only three. Sun doesn't come up for hours."

"Maybe some other time. Just let me hold you." Hunter squeezed her.

"No, seriously." She sat up straight. "I was surprised how freaked you were when you couldn't find it, and how mad you were at yourself for tossing it."

"It was a gift."

Alicia feared a previous relationship. Could she pry on the gamble that he would not pry back, and learn of Scott? The pit was back in her stomach. "An old girlfriend?"

Hunter laughed. "No. Not a girlfriend. Way back ... when I was born."

"Huh?"

"It was a special gift from my aunt ... actually my Mom's aunt ... my great aunt ... when I was baptized. But I never started to wear it every day until my communion."

Alicia liked the idea that Hunter spoke freely of his religion. Most guys didn't. And although she came from a Christian home, they rarely exhibited it outside of Christmas and Easter. "Your great aunt?"

"Yeah, she was a nun... Sister Isabel."

"Really?"

"Yeah, always dressed in the real old habit and all. She never changed, like the modern ones did. She was my grandmother's oldest sister. Everyone loved her so much and—"

Was?"

"She died my freshman year. Was a nun for 47 years. And I guess I wear it out of memory to her and deference to my Mom. I don't know. Maybe I'm just sentimental like that."

Alicia snuggled in silence, warmed by his honesty and tenderness. She was falling in love all right. It felt good.

"Brian's not coming back to the room tonight," he whispered.

"Why?"

"Cause Max had friends up from the city and a bunch of them are determined to crowd into one room and watch wrestling."

"And?"

"And I am so glad that the stupid drunken half-birthday night was not our first." He pressed her tight again. "I love you *so much*, and our first time *was* so special. I think of it all the time." He kissed her hair.

Alicia had tears and a contradictory ache in her heart, as she deliberately hid her face in his chest. "Me too.... Me too."

It was almost 5:30 a.m. when they fell asleep in each other's arms.

Four

"For those of you with little children, we want to remind you that there will be live ammunition fired. They may be frightened." Father Greg heeded the warning, as he likewise had to steel himself to ward off dire memories. Dennis Melrose, the paunchy veteran, whose coat displayed metals from both the Korean and Vietnam wars overtop a shirt, which did not fit anymore, made the announcement then stepped back beside the priest in the tent.

Paul Tuben, the funeral director, requested the few mourners present to stand for the rendering of honors. "Present Arms!" The fired volleys echoed up over the far hillside. Sounding a flat note or two in the playing of "Taps", the young bugler strained but no one seemed to mind. "Order Arms." Everyone sat.

Two foreign war Vets, one male and one female, proceeded to take the American flag from atop the coffin. Together they solemnly folded the lower stripped section

Jim Caldwell

lengthwise over the blue field.

As chaplain, Greg Pugh recalled his own training. The first fold represented a symbol of all life, the second, a belief in eternal life and so forth. Repeating to himself the prayer with which he ended his graveside remarks, *Dear Father in heaven, please give Duane peace in your everlasting presence,* the tall cleric became distracted. The decorated stole around his neck, made especially for him by the VFW troupe 386 ladies auxiliary for his burial duties, had become lopsided and Greg had his foot on part of it touching the ground. He adjusted it with both hands.

"There are three shell-casings placed into the folded flag for duty, honor and country." The next fold.

Greg looked at Dustin, Duane's only brother in the first row of wooden chairs. Most of the participants were members from their local chapter. The brother was the closest relative in addition to a cousin and two second cousins that Greg's secretary researched and could find in time for the funeral. The hardly seen sibling had a neutral expression and little emotion. Alone, he was unaccompanied either by his wife or his two grown children or their families. Everything seemed so obligatory. Greg felt downhearted that even in these final moments long held opinions could not be disbanded in lieu of respect for the dead.

Civil war tales would have referred to it as a blue-gray matter. Historians tell us that without lessons learned events are doomed to repeat. Mr. and Mrs. Harold Slubbler of Gaithersburg, Maryland lived it with their two sons. One was the draftee in the sixties, the other, the draft-dodger. One was the combatant; one was the protestor. One went to Vietnam; one went to Canada. The conflicted parents both died not seeing their children reconciled.

"Sir, this flag is presented on behalf of a grateful nation and the United States Army as a token of appreciation for your loved one's honorable ..."

Intersections

There must be others more worthy of receiving this flag, Greg thought, *like the Sweeney's or the Ruton's.* Each respective family took Duane into their homes upon Greg's request, each for a few months of a year before the nightmares and panic attacks became unbearable. The priest then petitioned his Franciscan superiors to allow Duane to live at the retreat house and have psychiatric help provided from the community's coffers.

What about even one of his three ex-wives? All of them were Vietnamese and unable to attend the funeral in the States. *They all tried, I'm sure.*

And kids? He's got to have kids somewhere. I know he must. Duane never mentioned any from the marriages... but all those extra dalliances searching for love... he has to have offspring somewhere. Law of averages without birth control. Anyone has to be more deserving than this guy. Whatever the situation, Father Greg breathed a sigh of relief that the man he first met in Saigon as a young soldier was finally at peace.

"How did things go?" The priest did not even have his coat or scarf off.

"Okay. It was a little chilly at the cemetery. The Veterans' plot is way up on the hill and the wind was somewhat strong in the tent."

"Duane was a sad story. He wasn't that old, was he, Father?"

"Only 46."

"Wow.... How did he die?"

Greg wasn't sure she could handle any gruesome details. He was curt. "Suicide."

"Oh. ...Hey, I have the next few weeks' schedule finalized. We have the marriage encounter with Fr. Joe Feely the week after Thanksgiving, and then the Silent retreat is the second week of December. And Billy is getting out the Advent banners to hang in the chapel today."

"Great."

"The mail is on your desk. And there are a couple of checks you need to sign for me." Apart from her age, Karen was very proficient and valuable in the office, better than her Mom. Eleanor Blesser had been secretary at the retreat house for years, long before Greg was assigned. When she announced her retirement, she asked him to consider her daughter for the position. The new director obliged and was quite satisfied with the younger Blesser's dedication and skills. Karen welcomed the opportunity to have a job just two miles from home with perks such as free parking and lunch, and the freedom to work alone.

"Thanks. I'll sign them and bring them out."

"And don't forget your counseling appointment at 7:30."

"Yeah, I'm okay."

Fr. Greg placed the ritual book back on the shelf behind the desk. The pages were worn. A veteran himself, he had performed maybe 20-30 military burials throughout his priesthood. Wherever he was stationed, he participated fully in the VFW. Someone experiencing the same atrocities of this highly disliked war could best minister to the aging Vietnam vets. His name was revered among local service men and women.

Mementos of his tour speckled the office. On the wall hung the letter of commendation from the top military chaplain and signed by President Johnson. In a picture frame on the desk was the frayed, purple stole, pressed and preserved behind glass. It was around his neck as he heard confessions that day he almost died. Greg placed the words from Psalm 90 between the two sides of the tiny vestment.

> *Before the (Marble) mountains were born*
> *before the earth or the world came to birth*
> *you were God from all eternity and forever.*
> *Teach us to count how few days we have*
> *And so gain wisdom of heart.*

Intersections

'Marble' was his addition. In front of it sat the miniature bottle of white sand gathered from the 'r&r' resort within view of the infamous site where death rained down. Together they symbolized death and life, destruction and hope. He often used them in counseling sessions to convey hope.

"Good God, another one!" Greg picked it from the pile. Like the other two, the only return address was three letters: Y.S.L. "This is getting out of hand. Someone needs help."

Disgusted, he sliced it open, skimming the badly typed page with a nervous apprehension someone has passing an accident. "Your baby brown eyes drive me absolutely crazy...it makes me want to do dirty things to myself..."

All three had the same form, a single crumpled page as though ripped forcefully from the typewriter upon completion. All had the "t's" barely visible and the "o's" filled in because of an old ribbon. Each escalated the licentious remarks. The first one Greg dismissed as a crude prank, but now the third one concerned him.

By no means was he a prude. Forgiving the sins of young men in war, being in a variety of parishes, being a skilled marriage and family counselor, he had heard the depths of lust and somewhat dysfunctional people. But now being the subject of it unnerved him as a man striving daily to be faithful to his religious vows. In a way, although the culture rarely spoke of it in terms of the male, this *was* sexual harassment.

"Your jet black hair ... your tall muscular body...your Adonis looking face ... if only I could be a fly on the wall in your shower ..."

It was someone who knew him. Approaching the upper forties, Greg had no gray hair yet. He exercised regularly. Ate right, and took care of his body; did not smoke. Drinking alcoholic beverages was only for celebrations.

"In my mind, I'm rubbing my hands over your whole body

and you would not have to force yourself on me ...I would willingly submit ..."

Oh, this person needs help. I have to tell someone about this and how can I figure out who this is? Have I encouraged this person to be so secretly passionate towards me? Is it someone I'm counseling?

Well trained, Greg knew that clients would sometimes transfer their feelings and fall in love with the person trying to help. But this went further. Love had no part in it. It was strictly sexual, almost pornographic.

"I would give anything to have you wrapped up and under my Christmas tree next month ... naked."

"Here, I brought you a hot cup of coffee." Karen stood in the doorway. Startled, Greg's face turned beet red as though he had been caught reading something he should not be. But they were sent to *him*! The priest clutched the letter close to his chest, shielding it from the young woman's eyes approaching the desk.

"Aaah... thanks", trailing off. "Mmmmm, I haven't signed the checks yet. But I will before I go to the Friary."

"No problem. I'm working on the song brochure for Fr. Tim's youth night. I just asked because one of them is due tomorrow."

Placing the mug down, Karen dallied as though she noticed that he was rattled and maybe would share it.

"I'll sign them. Don't worry."

She stood there.

"Thanks, Karen. That's all."

"Well," she hesitated, "I was wondering... aaah ... if I could talk to you about something."

Greg still safeguarded the letter. "What's that?"

"It's personal," she stammered, "nothing to do with work."

"Umm, do you think that would be a good idea? Or would you rather speak with Fr. Tim? I mean I'm your boss. It might get in the road of working with me everyday."

"I suppose, but..." Silence. Head down. She had no intention of leaving.

"Something at home ... with your family?"

"No."

"Something with your boyfriend?

"No."

"Something I've said or done to upset you?"

"No.... it's me."

It had reached a point of discovery. "Yeah?"

Head on her chin and almost whispering, Karen mumbled, "I'm having very bad bouts of depression... and loneliness ..."

Oh, my God, was she the letter writer? No, don't be stupid and jump to conclusions. But...

Greg recognized a counseling session with her wouldn't be wise. He was her boss. She had only been there a short while. "Perhaps, I could ask Fr. Tim to talk with you. Would that be okay?"

"I suppose." It wasn't a ringing agreement. The next silent minute was uncomfortable for both. "Yeah, if you would, please."

"I'll talk with him tonight."

"I hope you don't mind me bringing it up ... now and all?"

What did that mean, 'now and all'? Did she know he was reading the letter from the anonymous admirer?

"Oh, no. That's okay", the priest leaned towards her, speaking with a compassionate voice, still hiding the contents on the page in his hand, "we all deal with hurts and problems in life."

That was a dumb response!

"Sometimes it's just a phase, sometimes it very real and needs to be talked out."

God, he was automatically counseling without intending.

"I just think Fr. Tim would help you better."

"Okay."

Greg put his face into his free hand when she left.

Jim Caldwell

Ohhhh. Should I check her typewriter when she's not here? My word, I'm old enough to be her Dad. He could not read anymore.

Dinner with his brothers at the Friary was uneventful. Greg came late, having almost forgot his daily medication. There were five of them assigned there. Greg, Tim and Brother Martin staffed the retreat house. The others were part of the parish church attached on the same property. Alverno was an early 1900's mansion donated to the religious community upon the death of a philanthropic landowner from Harrisburg. Eleven miles from the capital, Alverno covered 20 acres of lush countryside across the Susquehanna River from Millersburg, Pennsylvania. Fulfilling Jesus' command to 'come apart from the world and worldly affairs to pray', Alverno was a spiritual oasis. The donor's will, in fact, stated the purpose of the gift was for "the Franciscan brothers to offer refuge to those struggling in the capital city."

The Order built an adjoining church, which served as a geographical parish for the better part of 15 years. St. Felix was a model of the post Vatican II liturgical architecture. And even though the retreat house had its own chapel, the staff often used the church for larger celebrations.

Fr. Greg Pugh was the fourth director in Alverno's history. Greatly expanding the programs during his short tenure, he added guest speakers and prayer groups and ecumenical retreats. His confrere, Fr. Tim McMannus brought a new direction in youth and young adult ministry. Diocesan and religious priests alike came from miles for quiet recollection and spiritual direction. And Greg's reputation for marriage counseling attracted a wider ministry.

But even the minister needs ministering to. Because Greg was the superior of the fraternal community, though, he would not share the letters with those under his charge.

But I do have to speak to Tim about Karen.

"Tim and I are going to the Mission on 12th Street in the

Capital to serve Thanksgiving dinner at noon next week. Anyone want to join us? All of you are welcome to go with us." Certain phrases from the latest letter haunted his thoughts. "And aaah," he lost his train of thought, "oh, yeah, that's right. The Provincial will be here the second week in January for visitation. Just in time for my birthday I might add." Everyone laughed. "We are first on his schedule for next year."

I have to ask someone how to handle it. Maybe I'll run it past Ray up at the seminary next week when I go to pray with Fr. Bede.

Vespers and night prayer were no better. Meditative recitation lends itself to the mind wandering. Words in the breviary, though not in reality, morphed to sentences from the letter on his desk.

How do I handle this? Oh, shake it off, Greg! But someone needs help.

Katherine Pelz wanted a divorce. Things had come to a head since the last session. She confirmed that Dave was having an affair. Caught him red-handed. And there was no turning back. No chance for reconciling, even for the two small children involved. The evening appointment bombed. Fr. Greg was an ineffective listener tonight.

Weary and tired, the pastor just wanted to sit and read quietly. A little spiritual reading might calm him. Perhaps jot some notes for next Sunday's homily should Fr. Mark ask him to take one of the masses at the parish. Maybe try today's paper or the current novel.

Military funerals inevitably disturbed his normally sanguine demeanor, most especially today's, not to mention the other matter from the mail. He struggled to wind down for bed. *The Jugger*, the most recent Richard Stark's crime fiction, could not completely dispel the day.

Jim Caldwell

Exhausted, Greg finally fell asleep.

He awakened violently a couple of hours later with the recurring dream, drenched in a clammy sweat.

It had been years since the last time he had it.

The priest sat alone in the dark.

Five

Russell reached towards Lynn on the left side of the table. "Pass the mashed potatoes."

"Say, please, Dad." There was a playful lilt in the perky adolescent's voice.

"Come on," he huffed, "pass them, I'm hungry." Realizing he was being rather negative for the big dinner, Russell, with his keen ability to change moods with a facial expression or simply relaxing his shoulder muscles, relented. "Please. And I'll need the gravy too, Hunter."

His daughter addressed the honored guest seated directly across from her. "Mom says you live in London."

"Sure do, hon."

"Aaah, I would *so love* to go to England. It's been my dream since I was a little girl" Her brother and sister, one beside her, the other across from her and beside Elena, both raised their eyebrows and groaned at having heard this fantasy a million times. Lynn paid no mind.

"Well, maybe ... if you Mom and Dad agree, we can arrange something next summer."

Julie interjected. "Actually she would like to go to art school in England."

"I could help find something there, too", accommodated Elena.

"Sure, like it would be any cheaper than it is here." Everyone chose to ignore Russell's pessimistic remark this time, not wishing to crimp the jovial spirit of Thanksgiving dinner.

It was Lonnie this time. "Mom says you two volunteered in Vietnam together after nursing school." Hunter was intrigued. Russell was eating with his head down. And Julie smiled proudly at the comment.

"Yes we did." Elena reached over and patted her friend's hand still holding her fork. "Your Mom and I have had some *great* memories." She was only looking at Julie. "A *lot* of good ones," Elena tapped twice again, "and some *not* so good."

"So, Hunter, I suppose you need a ride back on Sunday?" Russell pushed his plate away. This time the tone was neutral, non-expressive. "Or are you taking the bus?"

"Actually, I'm thinking of going up on Saturday. All I really need is a ride over to Erie. I'm going back with Charlie Manns. A bunch of us are getting back early for a party at Kyle's house in Rochester that night."

"Kyle?"

"A junior we know."

Julie spoke to the matter. "I can get you over to Erie, honey. Elena and I will ride you over."

"Good, mum."

Lonnie glibly trotted into the conversation. "Is *Alicia* coming back Saturday too?"

"I think ... err, I hope," Hunter said sheepishly yet bouncing gleefully on his chair at the mention of her name, "I think she's invited to the party."

The twins teased their older brother in unison. "Ohhhh, and when are we all going to meet this new *mysterious* girlfriend?"

"She's not *mysterious*." Julie and Elena enjoyed the exchange between her kids. Russell finished his cranberry. Hunter ate with his head lowered towards his plate. "I don't know, maybe some day."

"Christmas time?" Lonnie was relentless.

"Oh, I don't know." Hunter turned to Julie. "That's reminds me, Mom. I don't think I'll be here for New Years."

"Oh?"

"Alicia and her parents invited me up to their place for New Year's Eve and to stay a couple days."

"And where is that?" Russell asked again in a flat demeanor.

"Newark, New Jersey."

"Well, your mother's car won't be available. She goes back to work right after the first." He looked to Julie for confirmation, which he received with an affirmative nod.

"No, I wasn't going to ask for your car anyhow, Mom. I was planning on taking the bus."

"Okay, Hunter. Fine with me."

Russell shoved back to leave the table. His large frame projected a confident professional to any outsider's view. "I'll be downstairs in my study. I have some work to finish up on a court case for next week."

"But Dad, it's Thanksgiving." The girls again sang a duet.

"I know, but I'm behind." He leaned to peck Julie on the forehead. "Good meal." Elena perceived neither the tenor nor the kiss were sincere.

Hanging off to the side of the fireplace grate, the littlest log was only half burnt. Julie retrieved the poker and, with both hands pushing, nudged the charcoaled piece of wood back on top. There hung a slight smell of smoke in the room in front of it. She jiggled the damper a couple of times to assure it was completely opened. Flames licked from beneath with the gust of new oxygen to encircle all three pieces of the treated wood and produced a classic fireside picture. Julie returned to the sofa, curling her stocking feet under the blue and white Garrison afghan.

"Ohhhh, great meal, Jul. I can hardly move." Elena, slouching down in the opposite corner of the couch, held the plush throw pillow with both arms on her stomach. "I haven't had a good home meal like that for ... mmmm ... I don't know how long." She tightened her squeeze on the cushion. "God's knows I could never do that myself. Doctor I am, cook I'm not!" Both laughed.

"Goin' to see *Bettlejuice* at the Atlas with Cindy and Nanc and a couple others." The girls each kissed Julie and nodded to Elena. "Can Nanc come back with us and stay overnight?"

"Sure. Not too late, guys? No later than midnight. Maybe tomorrow all of you can convince your Dad to make his famous pancakes for breakfast like he used to?"

"That's a big maybe lately." It was amazing how often the identical twins answered or spoke at precisely the same time. "See ya." They did it again as they scurried from the room.

Elena followed the young teens out of the room with her eyes, pondering their answer to Julie's question. "My word, Julie, how do you ever keep them apart. I can't believe how absolutely identical they are in looks and personality."

"Oh, no. You're wrong on the personality bit. They're as different as night and day. And the looks, well a mother knows, I guess... little quirky moves, the way they react to things. I manage to somehow know."

Hunter tagged along within a minute. "I'm goin' to Nick's and a bunch of us are going out."

"Who's driving?"

"I am, mum."

"Remember. You have to watch the drinking now."

"I know, mum. Anyhow, it's my turn for the designated

one. I don't care. I just want to play some pool." He too kissed Julie. "Great meal. I'm stuffed." He extended his hand to Elena. "Nice to finally meet you. Growing up, we've all heard a lot about you." Little did he grasp Elena knew all about him before he was born.

"Be safe, honey, not too late."

Kicking her shoes off, Elena waved her feet in the direction of the fireplace, wiggling her toes. "It must be great to have those kids."

"Oh, they can be a handful, believe me."

"I'd take the chance." Her tone was plaintive but not remorseful.

"Would you like something to drink? Maybe another glass of that wine we had with the turkey?"

"Sounds good. Are you having some?"

"No, I don't feel like it."

"And you didn't have any at dinner. Not the Julie I remember." Her query was deliberate, as she looked down the sofa at her. Julie glared ahead into the fire.

"Oh, my stomach has been acting up the last week or so."

"Like at the Inn the other day?" Elena remarked. "I don't think it's your stomach. You *chose* not to have wine, didn't you?"

Julie was caught short. "Huh?"

"And you've been throwing up regularly, haven't you? I heard you again in the bathroom this morning."

Julie stammered. "Yeah, I've really been fighting something for awhile now. Nothing serious, believe me." She longed to change the subject.

"No, nothing serious, okay." Elena snuggled the pillow. "I know I've never been through it, but I do recognize morning sickness when I see it." Their eyes met this time. "You're pregnant, aren't you? And alcohol's not good when you're pregnant, is it?"

Crack! Snap!

Jim Caldwell

Two tiny hot embers shot straight up from the top piece of charred wood. The treated firewood retorted as though adding to the conflict. Julie rose, added two more logs, and poked both the burnt ones and the resulting ashes aimlessly. Her back to Elena, she was silent, lost in the fact that someone she had not be in touch with for years just stated a reality no one else in the Harrisson household knew yet. Julie turned slowly, teary-eyed and confused, but relieved she finally had someone to talk to.

"But I'm 43, Elena." They stared at each other. "What am I going to do?"

Together they gawked at the fire, each with their own thoughts. If the hearth could have transformed it would have become a TV set showing a rerun. Same scene, different time, far different surroundings. Two young women sitting in the warm sand, still giving up the day's heat, listening to the waves gently lapping near their bare feet. This occasion they shared a bottle of Chianti. There was sporadic gunfire in the far distance even though it was two in the morning. Behind them the large canvas tent rustled in the soft summer wind, inside the sometimes not-so-faint snoring of soldiers on army cots floated out into the night air. A few agitated and restless ones wandered up and down the shoreline near them.

"I'm goin' to ask to be transferred as fast as possible" was the secret then. The same question, "What else am I going to do?" was asked. Elena, then like now, had no real answer, only support and understanding.

She sought to calm her friend of these many years. "I know it's not what you planned, but people have babies in their forties and they do okay. We have advanced a lot in handling late pregnancies."

Julie slumped back in the corner of the sofa. Shivering a little despite being in front of a fireplace, she wrapped herself to her shoulders with the afghan. Again the two gave up their hidden emotions to the fireplace.

Intersections

"When did you find out?"

"Tuesday morning. I suspected it. I mean once you've had this experience, you know what's going on." She was compassionate even in her confusion. "I mean, I'm sorry ...you never ..." The two reached hands across the couch. It spoke more than words.

"I understand."

"My doctor confirmed it. Says I'm about seven weeks."

"Oh, the anniversary weekend."

Julie coughed a cynical little huff, speaking at the fireplace. "Yeah, after not making love for ages." Pulling the cover off, she quickly stood up and started from the room, throwing up her hands. "Surprise!" It was a facetious and uncanny change of mood. "Oh, well. Hey, I forgot you wanted another glass of wine."

Elena heard Russell conversing with her in the kitchen and the two appeared in the living room together. Julie carried the gold-rimmed goblet, offering it to her, and Russell had two pieces of pumpkin pie, one of which was his wife's.

"I'll be back with the coffee, Julie."

"He's finished downstairs?"

"Yeah. We'll talk later."

Hopkins airport in Cleveland was atrocious. Sunday night business travelers everywhere, not to mention the inimical returning crowd from the long holiday weekend. Julie and Elena sat in a couple of chairs luckily vacated right in front of them as they left the ticket counter. They dodged for them like drivers do when a coveted space opens in the parking lot.

The flight to LaGuardia would be slightly delayed. Surprise. Surprise. An airline late.

People, all ages, shapes, sizes, ethic origin, colors, dragging luggage likewise of all shapes and sizes provided a scrambled environment in which to wait. It was not very conducive to serious conversation, but...

"Here is my address and phone number. Please stay in touch if you need me." Elena handed Julie a small piece of stationary. "Call me collect. Anytime, if you just want to talk. Please. Let me help."

Julie blinked hard, taking the note. "Thanks. Somehow you manage to be there at the crucial times in my life, don't you?"

"Are you going to have the baby?"

"What are you saying?" Julie turned sour at the modern question. "If you mean am I going to have an abortion, the answer is absolutely not." She sat straight, pulling away. "Never. I couldn't do that, regardless of anything. No ... that's not even an option." Hands on her stomach. "That's a new life and I believe it." She didn't want to be so indignant since Elena was leaving.

"No, maybe I mean, are you going to *keep* the baby?" Elena was sorry she had offended her. "I mean, will you put it up for adoption or keep it?"

"I don't know. I can't think right now." Julie heard none of the fractious noise surrounding them. "But that's not the biggest problem right now." Grabbing Elena's arm strongly, "I *do* need to tell you something. I need to ask you something. I need your help."

"Okay."

"You know fertility and all that."

"Yeah."

Julie began to whimper oblivious to being in a public place. "Russell and I had a gigantic fight late last night. I didn't sleep at all after that."

"I heard." Elena spoke her confession. "Your guess room is too close to your bedroom."

"Did you hear the conversation?"

"No... no I just heard voices, but I could tell he was pretty irritated." Elena leaned closer. "You told him last night, didn't you?"

Intersections

"Yes."

"And he is not happy at all with the situation, is he?"

"No, but it's far more." All the stress lines creasing her face deepened, her brow furrowed. She clenched her teeth.

"Oh?"

Julie dropped her head and leaned into Elena. "I swear, Elena. I have never been with anyone else in our whole married life. And definitely not now, I swear ... I swear—"

"What are you talking about?" Elena lifted Julie with both hands. "What are you trying to say?"

A small five year old being dragged hastily by his mother to a departing plane fell right in front of them, dramatically cutting into the private dialogue. He was crying and the toy he was carrying broke in two. The mother swooped him and the wooden train pieces up in one try and continued rushing towards the gate. No one in the unruly crowd bothered to help. Julie and Elena were too absorbed to react.

"He said he'll get his things together. And he's moving out tomorrow."

"What!" Elena shook her head. "This is absolutely no place for this conversation. Why didn't you tell me in the car, or this morning before we left or something?"

"I wasn't going to tell you at all, but I need to get it out." Julie started to weep again and tilted over to lie on Elena's shoulder.

She didn't care that they were in an airport on the busiest night of the year. Perhaps a passenger here or there wondered at the sight of Julie crying with the other woman. But this was an airport. Departures make many people cry.

"He's leaving because of the baby?"

"He called me all kind of names, and accused me of having an affair. At first I couldn't understand the anger, the disbelief and then—""

"What?"

Julie pulled back again. "Funny," She wasn't looking at Elena. "I've suspected that *he's* been having an affair the

Jim Caldwell

past six months. ... someone from—"

All the tension between Russell and Julie now made sense. Elena held tight. The flight to New York was announced.

"He would leave because of the baby?"

"No, you don't understand."

Elena's flight was announced a second time.

"Russell told me last night that he's had a vasectomy." The last words were barely audible with Julie's head down so low, "sometime around mid-September."

Flight 734 to LaGuardia received the final call.

Six

Hunter stealthily approached Alicia from behind, wrapping his arms tightly around her waist and almost causing her to drop the plastic clothes bag she was carrying into Phiny Hall. "Ouuuu I missed you sooooo much this past week." He kissed her on the neck with his eyes closed.

Alicia enjoyed his warmth because she missed him just as much. "Hunter, you're going to make me drop this. Now if you really love me, you'll hold the door then go get the last box from my backseat for me."

"I'm so glad you came back today too. I was hopin'. Goin' to Kyle's with us?"

"No can do." Alicia kicked the partially opened door to her dorm room wide open. It was obvious that she had made several trips from the car as her bed was piled high. "I got the paper for Machinalt due Tuesday and I have lots to do. I was supposed to do it at home. But my cousins from Boston came and— well—"

Hunter dumped his box in the middle of the room and grabbed Alicia for another firm squeeze, pressing his whole body against hers. "Oh, screw Machinalt. This is still vacation 'til Monday."

"And fail biology for the semester. No way." She returned his affection, vigorously rubbing his hair as she spoke. "My Dad would have my head let alone what Machinalt would probably demand for a makeup." Alicia kissed him as a warm welcome, a kiss that said she felt for him as he did for her. "No, I got to stay here. It's my dumb fault for procrastinating so long."

Hunter shoved a small box on the bed to make room to plopped down. "But you've got all day tomorrow."

"Goin' need it," she pressed his cute dimple with her finger as she reached for the same little box Hunter had pushed away. "Reading tonight. Library's re-open tomorrow and I need to look up some things." She recalled her putting it off so long. "Lots of things!"

"It'll be open all day Monday too." Hunter grabbed her as she bent forward causing her to fall on top of him as he fell back on the bed. Face to face, they laughed and kissed playfully on the lips, on the nose, on the forehead, all over. Alicia mussed up his hair.

"Kyle's place is going to be a blast. Come on. Everybody's goin' to be there"

She loved lying on top of him. Pushing herself up with her arms on his chest, she asked, "How was your Thanksgiving?"

"Okay, I guess."

"I guess?"

"Oh, my Dad was being a jerk again." Hunter stretched to pull her down again for another intense kiss. "Something's going on there that I'm not sure of." Alicia paid little attention to his answer by pawing at him and then tickling with both hands. Out of control, he inadvertently kicked another box on the floor, laughing loudly and with one strong move, rolled Alicia over and was on top on her. "Got ya." He pinned her arms to the bed. "Now promise me, you'll come with us tonight." They wrestled like buddies instead of lovers. Hunter finally climbed off freeing her to also get off the bed.

"Ah, I honestly can't." She pleaded for understanding. "I'd love to be with you, but I got too much to do." Alicia added another argument. "Besides, I want to take advantage of the quiet with hardly no one back in the hall." She flipped a short wave at the other bed. "And Bev's not coming back 'til tomorrow night."

"Mmmmm, maybe I should just *stay* here."

Alicia pressed him away. "No! I need to be alone and get this dang thing done." Unclipping the clasp on her half-heart necklace from around her neck, she carefully laid it on the center on the desk. Hunter placed his hand on the complimentary other half of the heart ornament he wore on the same gold chain next to the cross. "Hey, did you get to the doctor over vacation?"

"Yea."

"*And*?"

"Got diabetes."

"WHAT!" Alicia reached into the air with open arms.

Hunter took it to mean surprise instead of alarm. "Yep! Seems I've developed diabetes. Reason I've been so thirsty and peeing like hell." He acted casual about it, making teasing gestures with his hands near his face. "I'm a type I" He laughed and mockingly laid his head on his right shoulder. "Just *your* type, I hope." He straightened up. "No. Seriously. Gettin' things started. I'll be okay. Nothing I can do about it, except take insulin and eat right and all that jazz. Should live to be a hundred."

"But—"

"But nothing." Hunter lowered her hands and pulled her closer. "I'm okay. Don't worry. People live with this all the time. However I am curious—" He wavered against the ensuing thought. "Oh, never mind. Hurry up and kiss me again. That will make me better."

Jim Caldwell

"Curious about what?"

"Later. Come on, go to the par--teeee..."

His girlfriend wasn't sure how to take his cavalier attitude. *Wasn't he concerned? Was he hiding it? Why was he acting like he just got over a bad cold rather than being diagnosed with a life long deal?* Alicia gave a strange look choosing to leave a more serious discussion to later. She started to undress.

"Okay!" Hunter piped, "And it's only seven-thirty in the evening."

"No, silly. I'm going to take a shower before I start reading."

"Darn." Hunter snapped his fingers. "And I thought I was about to get lucky."

Alicia pulled a white channel robe from a shopping bag on the floor and wrapped herself. Hunter trailed her as she opened a small purse-looking case and retrieved shampoo, brushes, body gel and other sundry items. "Now, walk me down the hall to the showers and get out of here."

He was persistent, hugging her and squashing the plastics bottles between them. "One last chance, you." He kissed her on her shoulder. "We're leaving in Brian's truck in a half hour. I'll still let you shower ... fast. Don't want you smelling between Brian and me in his clean truck." He broke loose laughing, using quotations marks in the air for the word, 'clean'.

Alicia hit him on the chest with the brush. "Ohhhh, you, yourself!" She headed for the door. "Seriously, Hunter, I can't go. Got to do this and get the stupid thing done. Maybe tomorrow night we can go to the Ratz or something. Everyone will be back." Behind her, he traipsed down the hall. Turning, she bopped him this time on the head with the same brush. "If I can get this done, I'll be ready to have fun tomorrow night." Reaching the showers, Hunter almost followed her in. She pushed him away up the hall. "Get goin'!" He laughed as he back stepped away.

Intersections

"Love ya," she yelled, echoing down the silent hallway. "Love ya!"

Diabetes? Mumbling, Alicia pulled the shower curtain open. *Wow.*

Phiny Hall's wooden floors creaked louder without anybody there to create human noise. Alicia rubbed her hair robustly, then cropped her long brown locks up into the towel and tied a knot to hold it in place. Picking up the pendant from the desk, she held it tight in her hand against her breast with the other one crossing over top of it. *Well, at least he knows what's been goin' on.* She was at the same level of love in their relationship, and it felt great. Alicia kissed the keepsake with the same affection as though she were kissing Hunter himself. *Oh, dang, I forgot to ask him if he's coming,* she thought, standing there clutching the charm piece, *for New Year's?*

Without changing, Alicia began putting things away. Clean sheets for her bed were next, and finally the bag of books she needed to tackle. She took the top one, laid it aside and reached for the one under it. Garrison University was dark, but peaceful and quiet.

"Hey, Bro want a beer?" Brian pointed the neck of his empty bottle as he passed the circle that Hunter mingled in.

"Nah. You get blasted. I'll drive," he answered as he took hold of Kyle's arm. "Hey, man, can I use your phone?"

"Sure. In the kitchen by the counter."

There were three gentle knocks on the door. Alicia had been absorbed the past two hours in her reading, not bothering to dress. She had to laugh at the thought that perhaps Hunter had chosen to come back earlier than planned. "I told you before. I'm busy, silly goose," she said through the door as she swiftly opened it.

Her face turned to stone.

The wall phone in Phiny Hall outside Alicia's room rang

and rang. Hunter twirled the cord impatiently as he waited. Ten rings, 11, 12 ... shifting his weight to the other foot. Fifteen ... 16. 20. He hung up. *That's strange.*

"Weeelll ... *Dee-Alici-ous!*" Scott leaned arrogantly against the wall, arms crossed and smirking. "Where the hell have you been, my love?"

"Oh, God!" Alicia went to shut the door. "I don't need you."

Scott blocked it with an upright hand. "No, the real question is: Do I need you?" He crudely grabbed his crotch. "And the answer is--" He pushed the door against her will. They struggled back and forth. A coed at the end of the hall, who had also returned early, left her room going towards the far staircase and paid no mind to the tussle at Alicia's door. Scott finally won, pushing into the room as she reluctantly backed up. Closing the door, he leaned against it, hands behind him, fumbling and twisting the knob to lock it. "Missed ya that Sunday night a couple of weeks ago," Scott fired at her as she tugged her robe tight with both hands and yanked on the tie around her waist. She still wore the towel on her head.

"Scott! I'm telling you. It's done with us. I really don't want anything more to do with you."

"I SAID I *missed* you that Sunday night," he was still leaning back against the door, "you stood me up."

Alicia held her ground, although fearful. "Look, I know, I gave myself to you. Probably something I'll always regret."

Scott frowned. "Really? You always told me you liked it as much as I did."

"No. It just happened and that's that." Turning, she removed the head towel and tossed it to her bed. "But, we're done." She caught a glimpse of the half-heart pendant on the desk beside her book. "Let's move on. It was just stupid sex with me. Nothing more and besides I'm beyond that."

Scott circled her like a lion does to its prey. "Stupid sex?

Really?"

Alicia followed him with her eyes. "Well, if you ever thought I felt something for you, you had it all wrong."

He feigned being slighted. Alicia sought to allay him with complimentary psychology. "Besides, you don't need me anymore. You have lots of others to have sex with." It worked.

"You've heard of my conquests I take it?" He said moving to stroke her face. Alicia pulled away. "I guess I'm just ...let's say ... *irresistible.*"

Alicia felt revulsion at his conceit. She pushed his chest with her upright palms aiming towards the door. "Let's just leave it there, okay Scott?"

Scott seized both her wrists. Alicia felt afraid. "But you OWE me."

"I don't *owe* you anything." Her stomach churned.

He was mean. "Oh, yes you do, *honey.*" This time he reached fast enough to be successful in seductively stroking her face. "You said you would be here, and you weren't." Alicia reached to remove his hand. Scott grabbed her wrist again sneering at her, "Nobody stands Scott Pincolior up and brags about it."

"I've never said anything to anyone."

"Well just in case," tightening his grip, "I don't want my *reputation ruined*," he scoffed, "and so I want what was promised that Sunday."

"Scott! You're hurting me!"

He strongly twisted and pushed as Alicia cringed and reacted to being pursued. "One last time, my pretty *Dee-Alici-ous.* A little graduation present for me since I'm done this semester."

The wall phone in the hall rang doggedly. Alicia hoped the girl down the hall had returned. She would scream for help. Scott was winning the contest of strength. He backed her to Beverly's bed with the ugly bare mattress. Alicia fell back on the bed from his thrusting and Scott came down on her just as fast. With his free hand he gripped her chin, then forcefully French kissed her with an undue violence, his tongue fighting to part her clenched teeth. The booze on his breath nauseated her. The weight of his body crushed her, almost suffocating her as he held her wrist down at her side. She was powerless, twisting her head from side to side in resistance.

"No! Scott. You bastard," she protested.

"Ouuuu, I like it when you're mad! You are really turning me on!" The phone in the hall stopped ringing.

"No! No!" Alicia struggled to push him off.

The harder she fought, the more strength Scott displayed. Still gripping her wrist for total control and straddling her body, he reached with his other hand to throw open her robe. With unbridled passion, he unbuttoned his jeans and unzipped.

"No! Please, no!"

No avail. The egotistical assailant had his way with her. As he panted with heavy breathing, Scott's eyes raged with selfish pleasure and power.

Hunter stood in the kitchen again. He let it ring 20 more times. *Damn. Where did she go? It's right there... near her door.* He resolved to try every 15 minutes 'till he got her. How he wished she were at the party. It wasn't fun without her! And Brian was drunk.

"Thanks ... for nothing." Scott adjusted his shirt into his pants and zippered up with a dominant arrogance that lifted him off his heels. "*Now* it's over. Because *I* say so, not *you*! *Now I* move on to a hell of a lot better."

Alicia was crying, sobbing, and clutching her robe as she curled in a fetal position. "You raped me," she muttered.

"I WHAT?" The tone was as condescending as ever.

"You raped me, and you're not going to get away with it."

"Who says?" He swung his arms around, "just you and

me here, babe. Your word against mine." The words dripped from his lips. "And as far as I'm concerned you were as willing as all the other times." The hall phone was incessant. Scott used it to bolster his argument. "Nobody's out there. Hear that phone?" He cupped his ear. "Anybody answering?" Callous and defiant, he glared at her. "No!" Supercilious again. "And I don't think the statue of Lady Knowledge and Science on the lawn outside there" he pointed at the window, "heard anything but moans from a willing partner, like all the other times you whored yourself."

Alicia buried her head into the musty old mattress with anger and disgust. "Get out of here, you son of a bitch! And I never want to see you again!" She screamed! "You bastard!"

Scott started to leave, still fixing his belt. "Ha! Now you get feisty! Needed that a little bit ago, *Dee-Alici-ous!* I had to do all the work. Stop it before you turn me on again!" He slammed the door, laughing scornfully. Immediately re-opening it as Alicia sobbed, Scott retorted in a matter-of-fact voice. "By the way, my sweets. I wasn't even here tonight. My roommate swears on a stack of bibles that I returned to school with him tomorrow night. Ha!" He swung the door wide. "Still no one in the hall that I can see. Ha! Bye, bitch!" He banged it a second time.

"Boy, you're cute, frat boy. Got a girlfriend?" The starry-eyed twenty-something swayed back and forth from the third mixture of wine and ginger ale she was downing.

"Definitely." Hunter answered gently breaking away to the kitchen for another try. *11:30. She's got to be back in Phiny.* He longed for her voice. The 10th ring succeeded.

"Hello" a low voice answered.

"Alicia."

She cradled the phone for the comfort of his voice. "Hi."

"You okay? I've called a number of times."

"Yeah. ... yeah I'm okay... fell asleep."

"Where were you earlier?"

"Aaah ... oh ... I went out to the quad for some air and got talking to some people."

"Who?"

"Didn't know them. I don't know ... some other juniors." Her answer was elusive.

"You sound like you've been crying?"

"No. ... Told you. I just woke up. And ... and I sort of don't feel good."

Hunter had a queasy feeling in his stomach.

"Brian's smashed. I'm goin' to drive back in about a half hour. I'll come over."

"No, Hunter. Not now. Not tonight. I'm *really* tired. I just want to go back to sleep. ... Please ... I'll feel better in the morning."

Alicia could still smell the overpowering odor of Scott's sweat on her face from when he forced a final repulsive kiss on her lips. She felt dirty and did not want to face Hunter in this state of mind.

"Aaah, I've read a lot. I'm exhausted." *Would she even tell him about tonight? It could change everything! Could she ever tell him?* Alicia's head swirled and pounded.

"But—"

"No, I'll see you tomorrow sometime. Okay?" Tears ran down her face as she hoped he would acquiesce.

"Okay." Hunter felt anxious.

The hallway was pitch black, except for two tiny nightlights spaced down the hall. Feeling very lonely, Alicia closed her dorm room door behind her and locked it.

Seven

The tip of the square bell tower on top of the main entrance appeared over the hill. Fr. Greg cracked a smile at the sight approaching St. Anthony Minor Seminary. To this day he remembered the apprehensions of a young, skinny eighth grade boy with brown-rimmed glasses driving with his parents in the mid fifties "to check things out" for the first time. Every rise on the six-mile journey out of York into the countryside revealed more and more of the well-built red brick buildings. Across the two-lane road was the massive ball field, next to the woods, where four baseball games could occur simultaneously without any interference with each other. Beyond the field the tiny lake had not yet frozen. Beside it existed the pavilion where shelter and hot chocolate warmed young schoolboys in ice skates, now and in days past. It needed a new roof.

Greg pulled into the adjacent parking lot, also used by the monastery residents on the grounds. The Friars living there taught and administered the high school & college seminary, as well as the local parish of St. Clare. Corney was

Jim Caldwell

the Guardian or superior of the community and taught English at the seminary.

Corney was Fr. Ray Sianti, Greg's best friend, closer to him than his own brother. Ray had entered the seminary a year ahead of Greg, a confident, funny sophomore who befriended the "skinny kid from the north side of Pittsburgh" the very first day at Anthony's. Both spent their teen, formative years laughing, competing and helping each other. Both entered the Order becoming Franciscan priests and continued to encourage each other.

Corney was the nickname everyone called him when Ray took Cornelius as his religious name in the Order. Anyone making vows had to take a new name, a biblical name, or a saint's name, a sign of a brand new life in the Lord. It likewise had to be unique, meaning you were the only Friar in that Province with that religious name. Ray chose Cornelius simply because it was available and it was biblical for 'horn' Said he liked "blowing his own". However, he never warmed to it and when the Second Vatican council in Rome suggested that religious men and women return to using their baptismal names instead of a religious name, Ray switched in a flash. The nickname stayed.

Corney knew everything about Greg, his family ties, his hopes, his fears, his life altering experiences in Vietnam. He stood beside him at the altar when he buried his parents; faithfully wrote when Greg was overseas and was forever constant in the good times and the bad.

In turn Greg knew the battles of Ray's life and priesthood including a cancer scare a few years ago as well as the time in D.C. when Ray struggled with leaving the priesthood for the love of a woman he met while helping at a suburban parish. During late night conversations downing a beer or two, they would comment on how life's unforeseen experiences so changed the two naïve seminarians whose biggest challenge then was opposing each other on the hand ball courts. The two men cherished their strong

Intersections

friendship.

The red-dog path above the same handball courts also required work. It brought to mind his school days on Fr. Roch's crew, replenishing the 'dog' each spring. Greg walked past the 20-foot stone cross, part of the Stations of the Cross, which encircled the woods. A little snow lay on the head of the dying Christ from a recent storm. Most of it had melted the past couple of days and it really wasn't that cold for mid-December.

Greg knew Fr. Bede would be in the woods, wrapped in the heavy wool cape, and not up at the house. He chose to spend time with his spiritual mentor before catching up with Corney. It had been months since he'd conversed with the elderly Friar, even though he had been to the seminary several times to golf with Ray and conducted a day of recollection for the students in early October. Having experienced the dream again, it was crucial to share it with his spiritual director.

The Fourth Station: Jesus Meets His Mother. Greg read the caption on the memorial as he rounded the path near the end of the woods before the open farmer's field with bits of cattle hay left here and there. How many times had he walked this path, encouraged as a young boy studying for the priesthood to "make the stations" during the days of Lent. Each monument was uniquely constructed from large stones, piled in an arc around an etched scene depicting that particular station, also in stone and indented into the structure. All were the same size and construction, except the large cross, number 12, by the main road.

Today, however, it wasn't those spiritual memories that flashed through his mind but rather the picture of a home sick adolescent crying his eyes out on the pathway down this end so "no one would see him and call him a sissy." The fair-haired, teenaged Greg Pugh sat that day a few yards behind this station not realizing someone approached out of nowhere to surprise him.

"Mmmm, why so sad?"

Greg jumped up, hastily wiping his eyes with his shirtsleeve. Ray had told him about the old priest, but he had yet to meet him. "Aaah, nothing, Father. I just got something in my eye."

The white-haired friar, almost doll-like, stood only about 5' 3'. He wore the familiar Franciscan brown habit. However, his garb always seemed darker than the other priests'. Perhaps it was because, unlike the others, he washed it so seldom as was the old country custom. Moreover, it was usually wrinkled from sitting on the bench, praying near the hermitage built for him in the woods. On cold days he pulled the hood attached to the habit up over his head for warmth, making him look like Ichabob Crane in the famous horror movie. The reclusive Friar spoke with a heavy German accent, in a low voice and not the commandant tones of someone in authority. He looked, from the viewpoint of the 13-year-old boy, to be antiquated.

Presently Fr. Bede was a fixture of the woods, an ascetic who once lived an active ministry but now was sickly having had the lobe of his left lung removed due to a severe case of pneumonia a few years ago. These days he spent his time in long prayer and meditation. And although it was fashionable to imitate his idiosyncrasy of rubbing his little goatee and opening every encounter with "how's your spiritual life, my son?" the seminarians revered and respected him as a very holy person. Most sought him out when they needed fatherly help, although few admitted it. Fr. Bede was a legend for the alumni of St. Anthony seminary.

Greg looked for the familiar figure among the barren trees. The brown of his habit meshed with the dull brown of the winter branches and practically camouflaged him. He sat hunched over, reading his new testament.

"Hi, Father Bede."

"Mmmm, Gregory. Hello. I haven't seen you for quite a

Intersections

while. And how is your spiritual life, my son?"

"Not as good as yours." Greg didn't really mean it the way it sounded.

And the old priest, in his humility, did not think the comment was funny. "Gregory," he tapped the bench, "come, sit. How have you been?"

"I need you to hear my confession, and then—"

"And then, Gregory?"

"I need to talk." He leaned closer. "I buried Duane Slubbler last month. He took his own life."

The bent over little man tugged at his straggly goatee as always. "I see. God have mercy on his soul."

"It caused me to have the dream again."

Fr. Bede tugged harder. "I am not surprised."

"It's been ages, almost nine years since the last incidence." Greg looked at the damp ground. "*Thank-God* it doesn't happen that often anymore. I couldn't bear to live with it."

"Mmmm, I can see that Duane's death would cause it to come back. Do you need to tell it again Gregory?"

The younger priest looked distraught like a specialist had just told him he needed major surgery.

Fr. Bede tugged. "You know when you have it, Gregory, it is the Lord's way of pounding some more of His love into you," he stroked faster, "like the blacksmith forming the shoe in the fire." The saintly man had used the analogy many times before.

"I know, Father, but it is so painful ... and it usually causes me to lose sleep for a numbers of nights."

"Gregory." Just the way the fatherly figure spoke his name soothed him. It had to be done.

However, Greg appeared embarrassed. He did not wish to convey that he only stopped to see the elderly confrere when he was in need of solace. "I apologize for not stopping down to pray with you the last few times I've visited."

"You are always in my thoughts, Gregory."

Jim Caldwell

The next 10 minutes Greg confessed his selfishness as the retreat house leader for letting Tim carry more of the burden than his fair share. Admitting his undue impatience with the other friars in the house he confessed also his lack of prayer and trust in God when he experienced this deep loneliness. The episode with the letters was not material here. That was something to discuss later with Ray. Fr. Bede, in the familiar, muffled, raspy voice gave the sacramental absolution, offering a penance to atone for his sinfulness and that of the entire world. Greg thanked him. Both sat silently.

"Gregory, was it as vivid as it has always been?"

"Yes, Father. It's as real as that day 22 years ago. I can see her face up close, her light brown eyes, and her haunting smile. Once more I feel the shock and confusion all over."

"How old was she again?"

Greg bit his lower lip, as the nervous panic in his belly usually started with the mere mention of her. The old priest knew the story well. But each time, he prodded Greg to say it out loud. This simple old man, who left Germany at the age of 14 to come to the States to study with the Franciscans, was better than any well-schooled, professional counselor.

"There is something healing in verbalizing it."

"Ten years old, maybe 11."

"And I would like you to tell me again, Gregory."

Greg placed his fists on his mouth, eyes closed, in a long silence, as though he were going to deny the request. Finally resigning himself, he rose and knelt on the ground. It was muddy from the recent snow, but Greg didn't care as he laid his forehead on the knee of the old hermit, reminiscent of the Pieta statue with the dying Jesus' head lying on his mother's lap. Strict German ways did not favor showing affection or touching another human being without great reason. But Fr. Bede suspended his cultural bent each time this man needed to re-tell the horror. He rested his hand on Greg's head.

"It was late June in Da Nang. I had been commissioned to travel that month in the area from platoon to platoon offering Mass and the Sacrament of Reconciliation. It was so rewarding to comfort those young men in their fear of dying and remind them of the Father's love like you have so often reminded me." Greg raised his head but was not looking at the old man; instead he was talking out into the crisp air as though he could see it all on some big movie screen somewhere in space. The mending began once more.

"Near the Marble Mountains, there was a large open field. They called it something but the name escapes me often. The 107th infantry patrolled there as the mountains with all its insidious caves were riffled with Vietcong seeking to kill Americans." He had tears.

"The corporal in charge of the base thought it necessary for the privacy of the sacrament to sit in the field, but not completely in the open. He placed me on a stool near the cornfield on the opposite side. I blessed and consoled one soldier after the other as they stealthily crisscrossed the field under cover." He wavered.

"Go on, Gregory." The staid man touched his arm tenderly.

"I had just finished giving Duane absolution and he was crossing back. She came out of the tall cornstalks." Tears streamed onto the musty habit of the comforter. "Her hair was shiny black ... and long ...down to her small shoulders, her brown face beamed with an innocent smile. She held the little box, decorated with elaborate Vietnamese artwork. I felt honored to be offered a present from a child. Out of the corner of my eye, I saw her mother in traditional dress edging her little daughter towards me. It was such a serene gesture for this frightful place. I thought God was showering a little peace in the midst of the wretched war. I was taken by her blamelessness and purity. She was beautiful." Greg stopped, wanting to quit the narrative.

Fr. Bede gave him time, uncharacteristically stroking his hand. "Go on, Gregory, you have to say it and let it out. It's okay to cry. They are tears of sorrow, not contrition. You did nothing wrong."

"I was reaching for the gift as she approached. Then—"

"Then, what, Gregory?"

"Everything went black. I don't remember!"

"Yes you do, Gregory, what happened? What did you see?"

He sobbed. "She got frightened when she saw Duane racing back towards me. I saw her trip …I saw her fall … as her mother ran back into the cornfield."

"And?"

"And I instinctively jumped to help. I would have died when the music box exploded had not Duane grabbed me, throwing me over his shoulder, as he ran across the field away from the blast. I looked back. There was nothing left of her sweet innocence except pieces of clothing… and limbs … everywhere on the ground." He was out of control, crying in front of Fr. Bede, sweating profusely in the cold air, shaking violently, still kneeling on the wet ground. The old man clutched him tight and let him cry.

Patiently waiting again, the old Friar finally spoke. "Evil is learned, my son, not born in us, except for original sin." His low voice calmed Greg even with its throated sound.

"But she was so small, and beautiful. How could a mother do that to her child?" He sobbed uncontrollably heaving up and down in the elder priest's embrace.

"I know, Gregory, war and hatred blind people. But I'm sure God holds her in his arms. Pray to see that the next time the dream comes. The picture of His love will heal it once and for all."

Kneeling there with his face buried in his own hands, Greg heard this many times before. But it had not yet happened.

"*When* will I see it, Father, *when*?" he pleaded.

"It will come. Be patient. In God's time, my son, in God's time."

The two remained silent for what seemed like an hour but was in reality only five, maybe six minutes. The comforter prayed without words, imposing his hand covered with brown age spots on Greg's head; the man kneeling underwent a spiritual catharsis once again.

Finally, they walked the remainder of the path back around speaking of lighter topics, and the old priest's failing health. Fr. Bede reminded Greg that the large granite twelfth station was the symbol of the Father's giving up His only Son to death for the sins of man's cruelty to man in war.

"Here's the fifth one, Corney." Greg handed his friend the last two letters he had received. "I got this just yesterday in the mail. Someone is sick."

"Oh, I don't know," Ray answered, "look at it this way. It's the curse again."

"What?"

Ray could not resist guffawing. "The curse of good looks that has plagued you and me." He laughed aloud.

"Corney, be serious. Someone needs help. How should I handle this?"

"I don't know. Pay attention to people often around you ... your prayer group, those who plan retreats with you, everyone. But I'll tell you now, it's not Karen."

"Yeah, I think you're right. No clue with her typewriter. I checked it."

"And I just sense that she sees you as more of a father to her than the object of some fantasies. At least that's what I've picked up the couple of times I've been there when she's been around."

"Yeah, I think so too. I just jumped to conclusions that day." Greg moved to leave. "Oh, well, got to run. I have an

8:00 appointment. Keep you posted. Come up over Christmas for dinner."

"Oh, I'm going to my relatives in Charlotte a few days between Christmas and New Years. Maybe early January."

"Okay, whatever."

Ray pointed half jokingly but also half seriously. "And that means even the little old ladies, Greg. You never know what the curse produces."

The light in Karen's office was still on when Greg pulled into his garage.

"You still here? What's going on?"

The young secretary pointed towards his office. The door was opened far enough to see someone sitting in the chair by the desk. "I didn't want to go and leave him in your office alone until you came home."

"Who is he?"

"Don't know. Walked in about 4 o'clock. Just asked if he could talk to you."

"Yeah?" Fr. Greg peered through the opening. A bulky man sat there in a dress uniform with a Green Service wool cap. The priest could not see his face shielded by the bullion visor.

"I told him I didn't really know what time you would be back. Said he didn't mind waiting" Karen shrugged. "What was I to do?"

"Did he give you his name?"

"No. And I didn't ask. Sorry."

"That's okay, Karen. Thanks for staying. Have a good night and tell your Mom I said hi."

"I'm Father Greg. You are?"

The man stood to greet him, removing the cap in a gesture of respect. He almost came up to the priest stature, slightly shorter. They were obviously around the same age. But the visitor was stocky, big built, like a retired football player. His hands were rough, his voice gravelly. He was balding.

"Bill Learney, Father, from the Department of Veterans Affairs in Washington D.C. I'm working on Duane Slubbler's Agent Orange case. I understand he died a few weeks ago."

Greg simply nodded.

"I think I knew him. I think we fought together in the first battle of Saigon in '68. I was also part of the 107th."

Eight

For anyone who has shared the experience of service for their country in wartime, there is an immediate bond that forms upon meeting. Greg led the man from the Veterans Affairs into the Friary's community room. "Would you like some coffee? I could brew a pot in no time." The business decorum of the office, plus its coldness this time of the night, seemed not to lend itself to this particular conversation.

"No, thank-you." The gentleman set the briefcase on the floor beside the plain brown leather chair. "But I wouldn't mind a glass of water," displaying two small white pills retrieved from his shirt pocket. Greg noticed the coarseness of his hands, the curve in his back as he straightened up, perhaps the result of an injury sustained in the war. The man brushed his suit coat with his palm below the decorated metals and ribbons before taking a seat.

Greg came back from the small kitchenette off from the Friar's common living space, handing the water to the unexpected guest. "Please excuse me just a moment while I reschedule the couple I was to meet with tonight. I believe I can catch them in time. It's a marriage preparation and I'm sure they wouldn't mind waiting until tomorrow evening."

Returning, Greg settled into the companion recliner opposite his visitor.

"Agent Orange case?"

"Yeah", the officer began, "since '79 the department's been actively seeking veterans exposed to Agent Orange or the many other herbicides heavily used in the theater."

"Used for what?"

"Destroy foliage which would give the enemy less cover as well as destroy their food sources. As a result many guys may have health complications for which there is compensation from an out-of-court settlement last year with the various chemical companies that supplied them."

"Such as?"

"Dow Chemical, Monsanto, Hercules, a place called the Diamond Shamrock Corporation and a few others."

"No. I'm sorry. I meant what sort of health complications?"

Bill Learney sat forward setting the empty glass on the table beside him. "Anything from skin or nerve disorders to certain cancers and some are even saying that it has caused their diabetes. But that's still being researched."

Greg reacted with raised eyebrows. "Well, ahhh ...why the name? What does Agent Orange mean?"

"Comes from the identifying color of the plastic bands around the 55-gallon drums." Bill stayed on the edge of the chair, leaning closer into Greg as though the information about to be shared was proprietary. "There were a series of toxins used by the military, the so-called 'rainbow herbicides'... white, purple, pink, green," his index finger counted them off in the air, "each marked with its appropriate color band." He simultaneously frowned and sighed. "Agent Orange was by far the most used, and perhaps the deadliest."

Greg folded his arms across his chest. "Mmmm."

"The studies continue yet today, and although there're probably many guys that were not affected, on the other hand there are quite a number that were. We think the government should help those service men obtain a just payment from the suit." He slid back into the chair and brushed his coat again, this time with both palms as though it were a nervous habit. "I mean mere exposure to Agent Orange or any other chemical does not automatically qualify any veteran to be remunerated. So, based on that, it is taking time to investigate and determine."

Greg scrunched his eyebrows, causing his eyes to squint as he listened with concerned interest, uncrossing himself with one hand hanging over the arm of the chair, his right elbow propped on the other and supporting his chin. He pushed against the floor with his foot rocking the recliner slightly back and forth.

"About four months ago or so when Duane's name crossed my desk I recognized him from the 107th." Bill hesitated. "I didn't know him that well, but talking to acquaintances who did, they all say he was a damn good soldier and most loyal to the corp." He caught himself for the slight curse word, as though the priest across from him had never heard it. "Sorry, Father."

"Duane *was* a good man! Too bad more people didn't know how good. Folks around here who never knew him before were afraid of him ... the spontaneous outbursts ... the scary fits of anger. But I was convinced he wasn't really to blame." He rocked a little faster with his response.

"Friends said he fought vigorously, partied just as hard and forever looked out for his combat buddies," Bill said.

The priest sat up quickly, raising his open hands into the air, elbows on both arms of the chair, as though praying at the liturgy. "You better believe it!" His voice filled with emotion. "Saved my life! ... literally!" The strong emphasis on the last word startled his visitor. "*I am here today because of Duane Slubbler!*"

Bill reacted to the disclosure by grabbing his knees and leaning forward, head tilted towards his host. Greg could see the discomfort on his face when he moved his back. "Really?"

Greg then recounted being a chaplain, and in particular the story of the field, the rigged music box, the rescue over which he had cried with Fr. Bede just hours before. Reliving it twice in the same day was uncanny. He did not dwell on the little girl, however, and stayed in control before his guest.

A short, plump Friar-Tuck looking man with a completely round face, the top clasp on his habit hanging open showing his white tee shirt and in bare feet swished briskly into the room. "Ohhhh, I'm sorry, Greg, I didn't know you had someone with you." Smiling broadly, he extended his hand in a most friendly manner. "Fr. Mark. Mark Romanitti. I'm the pastor of the parish here."

Bill jumped to attention as though a senior officer had come into their presence. "Bill Learney, Father. Nice to meet you. We're just talking about Duane."

"Mmmm, God rest his soul. Sad story indeed." Shaking his head, Mark turned to Greg. "Hey, I'm glad I caught you tonight. Can you take the 11:00 Sunday? Justin may not be back from his sister's in time for the weekend."

"Sure. No problem."

The vivacious Italian excused himself for the intrusion. "Thanks, Greg. Sorry to disturb you guys but I just wanted to grab today's newspaper," retrieving it from the table against the wall.

The two veterans sat silently for a moment of reflection together. "How long did Duane live with your community?"

"Well ... he's been in the area the last five years. Showed up out of nowhere. I *had* to help him. I owed him so much. Besides, I knew him too well and was aware how messed up he was inside. Got him a place and a job delivering for a local food distributor. He would come around periodically and report how he was doing." Greg scratched the back of his neck as he resumed rocking. "According to him, things were always fine but somehow I knew he couldn't handle it. They finally had to fire him. He missed too much, or came to work drunk which meant he couldn't drive."

"Friends from the retreat house tried taking him in, but that also proved to be too much. I eventually convinced my superior to allow him to live here on the grounds ... in one of the long-term guest rooms we have for friars from abroad studying here in the States."

"Was he able to work for you ... here ... at your place?"

"Yeah. But the poor guy had so many strikes against him." They both stared at the floor. "We tried. Had him doing odd jobs for us as best he could to give him some pride of working for his keep. But he tired easily and sometimes blacked out. ... I guess from booze ... we'd find him down and have to get him to his room. There were days when he was just totally unable to function in any way."

Greg continued, intertwining his hands in front of his shirt as though he were again praying. "But the panic attacks, the screaming in the night, the outbursts ... there's no way he could have lived on his own." He paused. "I guess it finally got to him when they diagnosed him with the prostate cancer."

"Oh?"

"Yes, early stages and they did say they could help him. But Duane was convinced he was imminently dying. Guess it was all just too much." Greg leaned forward, his arm across his lap, the opposite hand held open. "Ironic, isn't it. Here's a man who saved a lot of others from being killed and what's he do ... kills himself."

"Wow." Bill Learney was flabbergasted. "None of us at the Department knew that. The notice from you just said he died suddenly and nothing more." He couldn't resist asking,

Intersections

"How'd it happen?"

Greg spoke softly. "We found him up in the orchard," gesturing as though the visitor would know where the tree orchard was, "aimed a colt 45 into his mouth. Didn't even know he had it or else I definitely would have taken it from him." The priest sat back with more explanation. "Had him seeing a psychiatrist regularly and all ... but..." He trailed off, tossing up his hands. "Well ...what can you say? I have to believe that God has his reasons for things that happen, even when I don't understand them."

Bill closed his eyes a few seconds, and then opened, shaking his head. "God, the consequences of this stupidity we call war. Ordinary civilians don't really know, do they?"

Pursing his lips, he continued. "I have also been involved since last year with another project ... a program for homeless veterans ... those with psychiatric disorders ... substance abuse... like Duane ... I could have helped with some recompense... if I'd known," shrugging, "perhaps I should have come before this." He lowered his head, moving it from side to side. "God, there's so many sad stories."

Greg remained silent, the rocker pushed back, his feet up on their toes.

"Well, Father, any chance," Bill suddenly stood and motioned with open hands, "you know where his son is? Perhaps, at least, we can help him with some benefits in honor of Duane's memory."

"His *son*?" Greg hit the floor with his feet flat and jumped forward on the chair, caught off guard with the question, and staring up at Bill.

"Yeah. You didn't know he had a son?"

"No. Not at all," the priest was dumbfounded, "but I'm really not surprised. There was always so much mystery with Duane. Sometimes he told you everything ... other times he said very little ...had to wrestle most things out of him including the cancer diagnosis. He really kept everything bottled up."

Greg sat back again massaging his forehead in sheer astonishment, and asked "But how do *you* know he had a son? Cause ... honestly, he never said a thing to *anyone* around here about having any kids."

"He put it on the application when we first contacted him about the law suit and possible damages."

"Mmmmm, wow." The priest couldn't get over the thought. "A Vietnamese kid? I'm sure you're aware he was married to more than one woman over there."

"Yeah, that's all on the application too, three names, but I really can't say if one of them is the mother." Bill frowned. "Seemed to imply the boy is here in the States somewhere because he divulged the kid was illegitimate ... born out of wedlock. Perhaps that's why he was so reluctant in telling you." Learney explained what he could. "Gave no whereabouts but led us to believe that *he* knew where the kid was." Bill stepped forward. "Never said a thing, huh?"

"Would it make a difference if the boy were illegitimate?"

"No, not a bit."

Greg's mind was racing, slouching back in the lounger, stroking his cheek and rocking faster than ever. "Honest, he never said a word." Looking up, "What else do you know about this kid? I mean how old would he be?"

"I'm thinking in his late teens, early twenties. Duane cited an affair he had in the late sixties ... during a stay, he said, at the 'r&r' on China Beach. Said the nurse was pregnant and that it was his."

It was as though Bill had to clarify further, placing all 10 fingers on his chest. "I wasn't the one who interviewed him when he came in, but the officer who did made all these notes on the back of his application as Duane talked."

Greg's brow knitted.

"As I say, it's only a couple of months ago his application hit my desk. Government doesn't move that fast, sorry to say." Bill threw up his eyes. "Sometimes I wonder whom we're really helping. However, if this young man's under 18, or perhaps still under 23 and in school, he could be entitled to some rightful compensation as Duane's dependent."

He was still standing and pointed at Greg. "One of my reasons for coming here was to get more information from you. Duane gave your name as his only contact and this address as his residence. I just thought you would have more information for us."

"No, I'm blown away. And the brother and other relatives, whom we *were* able to locate for the funeral, said absolutely nothing. Although we really didn't have anything after the services." Greg contracted his eyebrows and lowered the corners of his mouth. "I wouldn't even know where to begin. Unless—"

"Yeah?" Bill stood almost at attention, hands on his hips.

"Unless I could help you locate some of the people from China Beach from that time. I spent about nine weeks myself recuperating there ... from the trauma of almost being killed and all."

Greg paused. "I *was* there one of the times Duane was. Got to admit, I was well aware of his wild shenanigans." He laughed a little. "Everyone was." He rubbed his chin, "perhaps that's when..."

Bill reached down opening the briefcase. "Well, Father, here's my card. If there's any way you can help, the Army and I would appreciate it." The switch to formality took Greg off guard again as he likewise rose.

"Sure. Whatever I can do. Duane obviously was very important to me." He placed his arm around Bill as he led him out. "Let me go through some things ... see if I can come up with anybody you might contact who would know more." They reached the door. "Will you be in over the holidays?"

"In and out, with a few days off. You can always leave a

message on my machine and I'll return your call."

Greg reached to the back of his neck again. "In all honesty, I've never really kept in touch with anyone there. Ahhh, when I returned back to the States and the Order, I made a conscious effort not to look back."

"Understand."

"But Duane was no help. His presence constantly reminded me of the past and that time."

The two veterans shook hands before parting.

Having missed praying compline, the last of the seven canonical hours of the day in the breviary, with the brothers, Greg opened the book in the privacy of his room. It had been an emotional day. His heart jumped in many directions and he needed some quiet and meditation.

China Beach. Good old China Beach.

The whispered words warmed him, and in a certain way, calmed him with the same love and concern shared so long ago in the midst of that personal travail. He clutched the breviary against his chest.

Tim McMannus knocked lightly on the door.

"Yes?"

"You okay? I saw the visitor in the uniform and was concerned. More about Duane?"

"He was from the Department of Veteran's Affairs. Said he had reason to believe that Duane had a son ... here in the States."

"Really!" Tim had the same reaction as Greg. "There wasn't anybody at the funeral."

"I promised to see if I could help locate him."

"Well, I just wanted to make sure you were okay." Tim held the door half opened. "Oh, and by the way, Karen and I have talked. She'll be okay. Just overly sensitive growing pains."

"Good. Thanks, Tim. I'm fine. Just tired."

Opening his closet, Greg moved a trunk and a box of

Intersections

books, reaching far back and retrieving the army green duffle bag lying against the wall. Having not been touched nor moved for years, it was covered with dust. The priest riffled in it past the old uniform and paraphernalia, retrieving the manila envelope filled with pictures and metals from his military tour. One by one Greg flipped through the aging and yellowing photographs piling them on the clerical book in his lap.

Ohhhh, China Beach.

He whispered again, smoothing one in particular, a group photo of the nurses and doctors in front of the large medical pavilion. He said the name of each one in the rows as he ran his fingers across it as though honoring each for their unselfish dedication.

China Beach. China Beach. China Beach

Greg softly repeated it over and over like an ancient ritual chant. It eventually soothed him to sleep in the chair as the prayer book and pictures fell to the floor.

Nine

Julie opened the three large boxes and carefully laid the ornaments on the coffee table, one by one. Each had its own nostalgia from past seasons. She put to one side the ones with dates inscribed on them, her and Russell's first Christmas together, the year the twins were born, the year they moved into this house in Mentor. She fingered others, each one with its own treasured story: a football with Hunter's name painted on it, bought on his fifth birthday and placed specifically by him on the tree each year until he turned eleven and decided he was more interested in music than sports; the popsicle-stick decorations made by the twins in kindergarten; the special little briefcase made for Russell the year he passed the bar exam; the tiny Santa Claus with Asian holiday artwork on his red suit Julie bought on an excursion to Saigon with Elena.

The house was quiet as the twins were staying at Nancy's house for the first night of vacation and Hunter had gone into the city. Russell called and asked him to have dinner with him. Said he had his gifts for him and the girls.

Intersections

At first Hunter was unwilling, still confused over the whole situation, but Julie convinced him to go.

"This is between your Dad and me," she said, "and not you two."

Only the soft Christmas music pervading the air and creating a festive mood along with the crackling of the fire could relieve the stress Julie felt approaching the days, which are constantly advertised as a special time of love and family.

Caught in past thoughts, she laughed with a little giggle as she spotted the favorite effervescent Christmas lights in the last box. *Oh, how the kids loved those dumb things*, she mused as she plugged them in to see if they still worked. *Always gave me a headache, but I loved to watch Hunter's eyes in particular as he waited patiently for them to bubble.* The telephone ruined the memory lane jaunt.

"Elena." Julie walked to the sofa from the kitchen with the portable phone. Their conversations had been long when she called. "I was hoping to talk to you tonight. If you didn't call, I was going to call you, but I never know how to determine the time over there. Its seven here, which makes it what there?"

"Midnight. We're five hours ahead."

"And you're still up?"

"Oh, you know me. I'm a night owl, like back at school."

Julie chuckled. "Not me. Age is definitely catching up with me. If I get past the 11:00 clock news, I'm up late. Especially now. I'm tiring a lot sooner."

"Cause you're sleeping for two. How you doin' with Linda?"

"Great. Told you before, I just love Dr. Murasko. Thanks for recommending her. Been goin' to her Cleveland office, which, ironically, is not that far from where Russell works. She has me on vitamins galore, to build up my strength. And she says everything seems to be going well with the baby."

"Good to hear. So, what are you doin' tonight? If it's as

cold and snowy there as here, I'll bet you have a great fire goin' and you are just sitting there staring at it."

"Oh, I've got a good fire goin'. But I'm not sittin'. I actually began to decorate the tree. The kids are all out and it so nice and quiet. And I needed something to try and get me in the mood. It's been a difficult year."

The lone string of retro C7 lights started bubbling vigorously on the floor. Julie decided to pull the plug as she talked. The fire also needed stoking. She cradled the phone between her cheek and her shoulder as she tended to both. "How have you been? Busy as always?"

"You know me. The busier the better. But—"

Julie thought the pause in the connection was due to the way she balanced the phone and adjusted her ear closer to the receiver.

"Spending time at Thanksgiving with you was *soooo* great. Therefore—"

"Yessss..."

"I've decided to take time off right after the first. How would you like someone from over the pond again?"

Julie was elated. "I'd *love* it! You are *most* welcome here ... *anytime*." She picked up a blue ball ornament that had rolled from the coffee table, but did not break, and carefully wedged it between two others for stability. "When do you say, after New Years?"

"Yeah, maybe early that first week, around the third of January. Okay with you?"

"Absolutely."

"Hunter's home I guess?"

"Yeah. He came home this past Tuesday. He's home 'til the middle of January." She corrected herself. "Well, actually, he not *home* that whole time. He's going to his girlfriend's parents' place in New Jersey for New Years ...'til the ninth or tenth. So you should see him before he goes back to school."

"How's he doin' with the diabetes?"

Intersections

"Taking it all in stride. No real major problem. My Hunter can be so laid back sometimes. That's the artist in him, I guess. He takes his insulin regularly and watches what he eats. The only problem I see is that he doesn't exercise as much as I think he should."

"And the twins?"

"As crazy as ever. They started their vacation today. They're staying overnight at one of their friends. And Hunter went to have dinner with Russell. So I'm here all alone."

"Dinner?"

Russell called yesterday. I just happened to answer. I usually wait as the girls run for it because it's always for them. It was actually one of the few times we've talked since he left." She hesitated. "And Elena, I have to tell you, it wasn't pretty. We sort of had it out."

"Really?"

"Yeah. He's told Hunter and the twins that the baby is not his and I was furious! This is between us two, and the kids should not be involved, let alone be told something like that! Crazy!"

"He said *that*?"

"He sure did." Julie was shaking her head as though they were talking in person. "I thought I knew him after all these years, but ... I just can't understand what's going on?" She lowered her voice. "I had to talk with the kids about what I asked you. It wasn't right, telling about how this thing happened between Russell and me. Discussing our sex life with my kids. Ohhhh!"

"What did you tell them?"

"Told them what you said. As delicately as I could I explained that a man's sperm could remain in his semen for as long as two months after a vasectomy. Wasn't easy saying such a thing, especially with the girls. But I had to prove to them somehow that I have always remained faithful to their Dad, and this *is* his baby!"

"How did they react?"

"What do you think? Embarrassed and confused. All three asked me why their Dad would say such a thing. I told them to ask him. I didn't know what to say. Imagine, talking vasectomy with our teenage kids. What was he thinking?"

Julie sought reassurance. "I mean, that is what you said, right?" Her voice took on a pleading. "I swear. I have never been unfaithful to Russell."

"I know. I know. I believe you. And yes, that's right. Although it is one of the best forms of birth control, with only about a one percent failure rate, still that eight weeks or so right afterwards a man can still be fertile. That's why most doctors have the patient come back and get tested for lack of sperm for a few weeks to be sure."

Elena then said something she would have gladly retracted if she could. "You guys played the odds right on the nose." It was flippant. She did not intend it to sound that way.

"Oh?"

"Sorry. I didn't mean it so be so cold. But your anniversary dalliance had all the proper timing and remaining— oh, you know what I saying." Elena was embarrassed and it came though her voice. "I mean, you could not have planned to put all the right factors together if you wanted to, you ovulating at the right time, him still fertile, unless-"

"Unless what?"

"Unless Russell never really did have a vasectomy."

"But he said he did."

"I know he did, but think of it this way. It sure is a *convenient way out* and would take away the guilt of an extramarital affair, like you suspect, off *his* shoulders and lay things on you."

Julie was disturbed and skeptical. "No, Russell wouldn't be that deceitful." Her tone exhibited, however, that she was questioning.

"Jul. When people get themselves into something they

know inside is wrong, they grasp at all kinds of rationalizations. They devise things that might even surprise themselves. Believe me. Been there."

The garage door opened. It changed the conversation on a dime. "Oh, Hunter's home. Listen, I'm anxious to see how things went with the dinner. Plus, with the girls gone, I'll finally have some time to spend with him. He seems stuck on this girl, Alicia, and I want to asked him more about her."

"And Jul—"

"What?"

"I don't want to sound like a parent but rather a friend—"

"Huh?"

"Jul, maybe this would be a good time to tell him."

"I don't know." She lowered her head. "Right now, with everything else going on …"

"There will always be something." Elena retorted softly. "Don't you think he should know? He's not a little kid anymore."

"I suppose … someday."

Elena decided to stop pushing. "Well, Jul, just a thought. Hey I want to wish you and the kids a very merry Christmas. And I'll call next week."

Hunter strode into the room carrying some wrapped presents and kissing her on the cheek.

"Merry Christmas to you too and please call as soon as you know your flight number," Julie said, finishing up the phone call, "and your arrival time. We can't wait to see you. Take care."

Hunter set the gifts on the end table "She's coming again?".

"Yeah, early January. She'll probably be here when you get back from New Jersey."

The phone rang in Julie's hands. "Hello." Her face lit up. Yes, he's right here. *Just* walked in." She shielded the receiver, a big smile on her face. "Speaking of … it's Alicia."

Hunter grinned as he took the phone and bounced from

the room for a little private time. "Hi."

The star for the top of the tree was not lighting. The tiny white bulb needed replaced. Julie rummaged through the opened boxes for a spare. Not finding one, she laid the burned out light aside on the same table beside the gifts as a reminder to buy one. She noticed it was an odd size but she should be able to find one in the Five and Dime. The store she patronized always added a special section this time of the year for just such needs.

There were three presents on the table that Hunter brought, all neatly tagged but none with her name. Julie was glad Russell remembered the kids but felt rejected at the same time that he had nothing for her. Despite the situation, she had bought something for him. It was already wrapped and somehow she planned to get it to him. *Should I invite him for Christmas dinner?* She thought. *What if he doesn't come? Then what? Should I ask the kids what to do?* The stress came back into her neck so she rolled it and decided to temporarily abandon the decorating and sit on the sofa with her feet stretched out.

The fire required attention. Tending to it, Julie returned to prop herself up once more on the couch. She could hear Hunter's voice in the other room talking to Alicia, but could not distinguish what he was saying. Her son laughed; he was quiet; his tone was light; his tone was soft. Julie thought at one time she heard him say he loved her. Closing her eyes, she smiled at the thought of young love. She saw it in his eyes. It was uplifting despite the constant ache in her own heart.

"Lonnie called while I was on the phone with Alicia. The three of them are going bowling and they just wanted you to know. They're staying the night, aren't they?"

"Yes. So it gives me some special time with my favorite son," Julie said with a lilt, beckoning him to sit. Hunter lifted her legs, parked himself on that end of the sofa, and placed her stocking feet on his lap, massaging her toes.

"Oh, do that for a million years." Julie quieted. "How was Dad?"

"Okay, I guess. I asked him why he didn't have a gift for you. He didn't really answer me."

"Oh, that's okay honey. It's not between you and Dad. It's between us. It doesn't matter, not having a gift. I'll get over it." It did matter inside her heart. "Did you have a nice dinner?"

"So-so. I had roast beef. It was okay, but I'm not big on that restaurant in his building. As usual he was soooo busy and was *squeezing* this in... yet he invited me."

"Oh, honey, don't be so cynical. Sometimes a professional is very busy. Your Dad's a good lawyer and helps a lot of people."

"So what if he messes up our lives."

"Hunter, take it easy. It'll work out. You'll see when the baby comes." Julie didn't want him to be so dismayed and affected by the whole situation.

But he was.

Leaning back she nicely changed the subject. "How's Alicia?"

"Good."

"You get your plans confirmed?"

"Yeah. I'm going out the morning of News Years Eve. I'll probably stay 'til the tenth. Her folks have some things planned. Like skiing ... I can't wait. Her Dad belongs to this lodge. Should be fun. I've never skied before." He looked up. "Think I'll get my tickets tomorrow."

Julie was anxious to ask more. "You really love her, don't you?"

Hunter smiled at the fire, at the very though of being in love, and precisely at the idea that his Mom asked. He turned to face her. "I do, Mom. She's just so good looking ... and funny ...and warm...and..."

"How did you guys meet?"

"We were in an English Lit' class together last year. Just

started joking around. Professor Harkins paired us together to lead a discussion group project and we had a ball." He was beaming from ear to ear. "In September, I couldn't wait to see her after the summer."

"Do you think she's the one?"

Hunter was caught unaware by the question. "Oh, I don't know." He laid his head on the top back of the sofa and remained quiet awhile. "Maybe. I do know this. I've never felt this way with anyone else. I mean I really feel great around her." As usual the fire interrupted the conversation as it crackled and spit sparks. "I mean, I want her to be the one but—"

"But what, honey?"

"As much fun as she can be, there still so much mystery sometimes that I don't understand."

"There's always mystery in people, Hunter. That's the joy in falling in love, spending a lifetime learning more and more about the other person." Julie turned her head away. "Even unforeseen things and surprises as it goes... that's the stuff of life."

"You mean like a pregnancy in late life with no support from the father?"

Julie gasped slightly at his pessimism, attempting to allay his negative feelings by changing the topic. "So, what do you think about having a little brother or sister 20 some years younger than you?"

"I think its cool." He hesitated.

Julie waited.

"I just wish Dad would provide for you the way he should." He rose and stoked the fire. "I mean, Mom, if I were to be in that situation" he spoke with his back to her, "I think I would immediately take responsibility for my actions."

Julie waited some more.

"Isn't that's what Dad always taught me?" He turned to her with a painful look, "so why is he not here now?"

Intersections

"I don't know, Hunter. I just don't know. Call me naïve, but I have an optimistic feeling that everything's goin' to be okay. My main objective now is to take care of myself and bring a healthy baby into this world."

Hunter hugged her. "I love you, Mom. And by the way, it better be a little brother to even things out in this family." Both laughed as Julie rubbed her stomach and her son pointed in that same direction.

Noticing the bubble Christmas lights Hunter had the same reaction his Mom remembered laying them out. "Oh, these things. We haven't put these on the tree for years." He challenged Julie in a playful way, pulling her up from the sofa. "Come on, let's put them on this year. Just for old times' sake. The girls will go bananas."

They wound them around the very bottom of the tree. "But don't forget. I never trusted these things. We can't leave the tree lights on without being around. I never did think they were safe, like the newer ones today."

Together they strung the other lights and hung ornaments. "The star has to wait 'til I get a new bulb." They spent an hour decorating before Julie astonished him with another question. "How's about a glass of wine with your Mom?"

Hunter had never shared a drink with either of his folks. "But you're pregnant." It sounded strange for a 21-year-old son to say that to his mother.

"One little glass wouldn't hurt either one of us. Besides it's almost Christmas and I'm enjoying time with my son and–" She trailed off catching herself as she almost admitted she needed a confidence booster to share something he should know.

"Okay."

Julie did the honors offering Hunter his wine as they both sat before a revived and very hot fire. "I'm so happy for you, honey ... finding Alicia and all. When are we goin' to meet her?"

"I was thinking I'd ask her to come here for spring break."

"Oh, that'd be great. Are her folks nice?"

"Very nice. I've met them a couple of times at school. Her Dad's a counselor of some sort. Not exactly sure what, but they are very nice. I'm looking forward to it, unless—"

"What?"

"Unless there's something changing between Alicia and me."

"What do you mean?"

"Like I said before, I love her so much but there're things that worry me. She's always so bubbly one time and then at other times, she's moody."

"Aren't we all?"

"Yeah, but—" He drank some of his wine. "Like things were great and then something seemed different the last two weeks or so before we came home."

"Maybe she was just preoccupied with tests and all. You were, weren't you? "

"Yeah, but," he shrugged, "I don't know."

"How was she now … on the phone?"

"Great. She wanted to make sure I was coming. Said she can't wait. Sounded like the fun Alicia and—"

"And?"

"And she told me she loves me." He blushed a little sharing this with his Mom, but thoroughly enjoying the butterfly excitement inside along with the relaxation from the wine. He slouched down laying his head back, smiling.

Julie finished her wine and leaned to tap him on the arm. "See, it will be okay. I'm so happy for you. Just be cool and let your love grow. Take lots of time getting to know each other." She sounded like a mother. "When she needs time to be quiet, let her. When she's sad, be sad with her. When she's happy, be happy with her. Just let it happen." She bent over all the way and kissed him on the cheek. "I love seeing you happy."

Intersections

The bubble lights warmed up as they had plugged in the tree. "Hey, look." Hunter sounded like that five-year-old who was so taken with the 'new' lights.

Julie did not want to do what she knew she had to. The atmosphere was right. The time was ripe.

"Hunter."

"Yes, Mom."

"I'm so glad we have this time together, just you and I." She paused. Hunter looked puzzled. "I don't get much time with you being away and the girls being around and—"

"What Mom?"

"Well, there's something I want to tell you."

Hunter was sure it involved the tension between his parents and what he had said before. He played with his wine glass, not looking at her. The fireplace quieted as though it knew what was coming.

Julie had her index finger ringing the rim of the wine glass, looking into the hearth for the right words to start. Her face was flushed both from the fire and the nervousness of what she needed to relate. "Remember how I said before that life can take funny twists ... that's sometimes we may do something we might regret later..." She straightened up, looking at the grate as though talking only to herself and not to him, almost sounding indignant. "No, I take that back. There's absolutely nothing about what I need to say that I regret. No. Nothing."

Hunter was positive now it was about the present situation between his folks. He sat quietly waiting.

"Well –"

The phone could not have rung at a worst time. Hunter jumped to answer it. Julie sat dumbfounded not knowing how to handle being interrupted at precisely the one time she had come to the brink of telling him.

Hunter retuned, the telephone held against his chest. "It's for you, Mom."

"Who is it?"

"Says he from the Department of Veterans Affairs" He did not give it to her immediately. "But, first, what did you want to tell me?"

At the very thought of a bureaucrat from the past contacting her, Julie's insides reacted with a swift shot of adrenaline tingling through her whole nervous system. Her mind raced with possibilities.

I can't believe the timing!

She sighed as she reached up to hug him. "I'll tell you later, honey. I promise," she whispered,

"Funny, he asked for you by your maiden name."

Ten

Linda Murasko washed her hands at the small sink in the corner as Julie swung her feet from the stirrups and sat on the side of the table. "Everything looks great, Julie. But there are a couple of items to go over with you. Please finish dressing and let's sit in the office a bit."

The plaque on the desk depicting varied stages of pregnancy in a cut-away womb reminded Julie of the fascinating experience she had had twice already and yet was brand new. "Julie, you are aware that an advanced age pregnancy brings greater risks." Any patient would have winced at the term, 'advanced age', had Linda not been so professional in her demeanor and tone. "For instance, after the age of 40 the possibility of a miscarriage could double in some women." Julie shook her head to acknowledge she was aware of the higher percentage. "And there's always an increased tendency to develop high blood pressure," she smiled to assure that this did not seem apparent in Julie's case, "but with that all said, I don't feel there are any problems here. You know how to take care of yourself by eating right and getting plenty of rest." She flipped her hand with the next statement as though it were just a woman-to-woman discourse. "Don't worry about that dust on things in the house. Ask the girls to do more. And Hunter too. I'm sure they'll be a big help now when you need it."

"Oh, they've been great so far. All three of them are treating me too cautiously, like a glass doll that will break or something."

"Good. But there is something else I want to bring up."

Julie straightened in her chair.

"Another risk that comes with a pregnancy later in life," -- the phase this time did not sound as menacing as 'advanced age' – "is the possibility of a Down syndrome baby. If it's okay, I would like to schedule an amniocentesis. This is an ultrasound procedure that—"

"I know what it is, doctor. However, that wouldn't be necessary."

"Well, I need to discuss it in case you would wish to abort should there be something wrong. This would be the time."

"Doesn't matter if my child would have Down syndrome or not. Abortion is not an option for me and I would accept whatever happens."

"Okay, Julie. Its part of my job."

"I know."

Dr. Murasko rose, extending her hand. "Well, then, as I say things are going fine. Continue taking the vitamins and rest and I'll see you next month unless you need me sooner." Coming around the front of the desk, she ushered her out. "Marion will schedule you."

There was a nervous apprehension in the pit of her stomach as Julie entered Russell's building with the long, narrow, ornate lobby, high priced shops running up and down both sides. The horde of shoppers jostled each other, and not in a friendly manner despite bell-ringers at red

Intersections

kettles requesting charitable contributions for those not as fortunate at Christmas time. Holiday music wafted through the atrium to lure the consumers into the retail establishments. Julie squashed into the elevator.

On the glass door of Russell's firm on the 23rd floor, she immediately discerned that one name had been removed and there were now only four lawyers named. They were listed alphabetically. Her husband's name was the second one. Richard Conroy was deleted. Julie and Russell had often dined with Rich and his wife and the absence of his name struck her since nothing about his leaving the partnership had ever been mentioned in the preceding months.

As few times as Julie had been to the office, she never ceased to be overwhelmed by the opulence of the paneling, the furniture, the ambiance of a highly successful group of lawyers. Artwork depicting a contemporary style hung on two of the walls of the small but rather inviting reception area. Brochures about wills and probate cases and the need for an attorney even in the case of 'small claims court' lay in perfect order on the two end tables beside leather chairs. Tall lamps with fashionable light tan shades were lit, adding welcomed warmth to what could be a staid legal atmosphere.

Julie and her family led a more simple life than what was present here in the city. The business had grown since her last visit nearly a year ago. And since she made it a practice in their lives rarely to bother Russell at work, Julie was again amazed. The firm now had three paralegals scurrying here and there with papers and memos and a new receptionist at the front desk, whom she did not recognize.

"Mr. Harrisson, please."

"And whom should I say is here?" The question caught Julie off guard not so much from the young woman's asking as to her response.

"His wife," she said timidly.

"Oh, Mrs. Harrisson. Nice to meet you." She rose from behind the desk and reached. "I'm Danielle Cowles. Nice to meet you. I'll let him know right away that you are here." Instead of simply buzzing Russell on the intercom, she walked away to announce her in person.

Julie noticed Danielle wore her skirt a little too tight for the setting and her newly purchased high heels appeared to be causing some discomfort as she walked down the long hall and disappeared around the corner. Russell occupied the second largest office on the south end of the building, overlooking the square. Julie sat, earnestly clutching the brown paper bag with the wrapped Christmas present for her husband, until the bright receptionist summoned her with a wave from down the corridor.

Russell did not stand as she entered, hiding behind the desk as if it were a fortress to protect from the volleys of an enemy. Julie noted immediately the newly dyed hairstyle and contacts in place of his dark rimmed eyeglasses. She chose not to acknowledge it.

"Hello."

"Hello."

The tenor was flat, neutral, and non-committal. His shoulders stiffened; his hands wedged between the top drawer and his body, Russell gave the impression he was more irritated with the visit than surprised.

"What do you want?"

"Sorry to bother you here but I was just at my obstetrician's office down the street and needed to confirm something."

"Oh?" Raising one hand to grip his chin and cover his mouth he rested his elbow on the desk pad, scarcely reacting to the idea of a doctor's appointment. "What?"

He never asked how she was nor motioned her to sit. Julie took the initiative taking one of the two high back chairs immediately in front of the desk. Scanning the room, she observed the marks of a licensed attorney, the enormous legal stack along the whole back wall, the small, round table for consultation and paper work to the side, the wet bar for informal meetings and settlements.

The place was better described as three rooms in one. Near the bar sat a flowered settee and a rectangular coffee table with a little red corvette lighter smack in the middle, nothing else cluttering the top. Back in the early days of the practice when Russell still smoked Julie bought him the curio as an office-warming present. Behind the well-stocked bar were keepsakes from past college days and favorite sports teams placed here and there among the miniature bottles.

What grabbed Julie's attention most of all were the pictures on the credenza behind Russell. Hunter's high school graduation picture had a snapshot of him clowning around with three of his friends at Garrison tucked at an angle in the bottom of the frame. Lonnie posed in her cheerleading outfit from Mentor High; Lynn's picture was a shot from a cousin's wedding last year. But Julie's portrait as well as their wedding picture was missing. One more barb to stab her heart as she sat respectfully before her estranged spouse. The baby budged from the tension.

"What happened to Rich Conroy?" Maybe some dialogue would help break the ice obviously frozen between them.

"Moved to Florida."

"Florida?" Julie felt Russell's aggravation with her presence. "Why? The kids are still in high school, aren't they? And doesn't she teach math in the middle school? How could they leave in the middle of the school year?"

"Divorced."

"Divorced?" Julie's inflection demonstrated total shock. When?"

"Finalized a month ago."

"You mean it's been going on a long time?"

"About a year."

"Really!" she blinked three times fast. "Well, how *is*

Noreen?"

"Don't know."

The staccato answers did nothing but add to his coldness. The fact that she knew nothing of their friends' failed marriage and the idea that Russell showed no concern for Noreen left Julie flummoxed and speechless, cutting her off from pursuing their story. She leaned her chin down on the top of the parcel held in her folded arms.

The real purpose of her visit stumbled out. "Listen, is there a new medical insurance number?"

"Yes, we recently changed providers."

"Well, thanks for telling me," Julie said sarcastically. "I *will* need the new information. At my doctor's office, I was quite embarrassed when they informed me there was a problem with my card."

"Okay, I'll have someone send you the new information and so forth." His tone was so lifeless; it was as though he were chatting with the clerk at the confectionary across the street while reading his daily newspaper. However, he did concede a little remorse for not updating her. "Sorry, I should have told you."

Julie's head swirled. So many things she wanted to say, so many questions to ask whose answers she did not want, a massive void between them. "Hunter said you two had a nice dinner."

"We did."

"He's all excited about going to New Jersey for News Years."

"Good."

"And the girls send their love." Julie said this not knowing whether they said it or not.

"Okay." Answers were monotone and as short as possible.

"Russell." Julie needed to know.

"Yes?"

"Where is this going?"

Intersections

"Where is what going?"

"You and me?"

"Yeah?"

"I mean are we going to follow the Conroys? Are *we* at a point of no return? I mean what's going on here?" She licked her dry lips, feeling as panicky in this state of affairs as a high school freshman being scolded by an ominous principle for wrongdoing, which she did not do. The baby inside kicked. "Are we also heading for a divorce?"

Before any single word answer came from Russell, a stylish, tall woman in her mid-thirties, dressed in a suave black and white business suit, a ruffled light yellow blouse and carrying a manila folder knocked on the door, opening it as she did.

"Hey, Russ, ahhh I mean Mr. Harrisson, sorry. I didn't know you were busy. But here is the Tully case that you'll need to study for this afternoon's conference with their attorneys."

Russ? He always wanted to be called Russell.

Julie caught the informality immediately. *Was this her? The one she suspected was the cause of everything?* She analyzed her approach to his desk, her bold manner as she bent over to address Russell, and the strong eye contact between the two. *Was she the one who had her husband's head all screwed up?* Her own head reeled; there was a pit in her stomach, her mouth had a sour taste.

Was she really meeting the woman who might be breaking up their marriage of 20 years? Did she imagine it or was there affection in his answers to this business associate? Julie observed the woman's shapely figure, her firm bust, her smooth skin and facial features, her appearance as though she had just climbed out of a cosmetic commercial. Julie whiffed her perfume as the other female past, seductive –yes, but not overpowering for an office environment. And right now, in her vulnerable state, she was absolutely no competition to this woman for

Russell's attention.

Really, was this person the object of her husband's mid life crisis?

"Thank-you, Christine. I'm pretty sure I'll be ready." Russell smiled at her with direct eye-to-eye communication, something he denied Julie. The non-verbal signs in this exchange bothered her more than what was said.

Christine.

"I don't know yet." Russell answered Julie without any hesitation when the posh paralegal exited as though there had been no interruption. "I'm still spinning from the fact that you're having a baby at your age."

"My Age?" Julie did not want a confrontation, but resented the 'age' remark as though she was somehow so much older. She refused to shy from the truth. "Our baby!"

"Whatever," Russell flipped not wanting to quarrel at this meeting, "but I'll say it again. I doubt it's mine." He never looked at her.

"Yes it is and you know it!"

"Whatever. Anything else?" turning back from glaring out the large windows, "I'm very busy."

Julie stiffened at the subtle rebuke. She rose slowly. "No, that's all I needed, just the new insurance number." Her back to him, she became annoyed after seeing whom she considered the other woman. "You can deny it's your baby, but you can't deny I'm still your wife and you have to provide medical help." Her voice was biting and displayed a subtle threat. "Surely, *you know* the legal consequences if you don't!"

Hating her own pessimism, Julie softened somewhat "We'll let the future sift itself out. In the meantime, I strongly suggest you talk to someone about your mid life crises and this semi-legal bimbo of yours." She waved towards the door that Christine had recently gone out.

Russell took umbrage at her words, scowling but remaining strangely silent.

Intersections

Julie reached the door and turned, holding out the wrapped object in the paper container she had cradled through the whole encounter. The total awkwardness and confusion of this meeting was not more evident than in Julie's attitude reverting to kindness after having been so stinging. "I brought your Christmas present." She moved to the right and laid it on the edge of the bar, sack and all, without looking back at him. Russell said nothing.

Julie left the towers, shaken and distraught at having never gotten to the point of inviting him for Christmas dinner nor telling him about Duane Slubbler taking his life.

Russell sat fighting with his pen on the legal pad lying in front of him, stabbing it forcefully in anger and frustration. Shoving the file aside that Christine had brought, he laid his head down on the desk for a long silence. Danielle buzzed him twice for answers to questions she had concerning a brief she was typing for him, and phone calls. Russell ignored the intercom. She took it that Russell was not to be disturbed during the visit with his wife. Danielle had not seen Julie leave.

With dismal emotion, Russell poured a shot glass of bourbon from the bar and downed it in one swallow. He locked the office door and poured another one. Sullen, he wheeled one of the chairs with rollers from the conference table nearer the corner picture window overlooking Cleveland.

Below, multitudes bustled here and there for final holiday shopping. The tall Christmas tree in the square captured the gaze of many, especially little ones who clung securely to their parents. He could see at least three more Salvation Army volunteers and their tripod kettles in front of various establishments.

Disconcerted, Russell retrieved the 8 X 10 wedding portrait from within the credenza. Within seconds he slammed it face down again and pushed the drawer closed with a sulk.

Jim Caldwell

The city was ablaze with activity; music blared from the speakers outside any number of the department stores.
It's beginning to look a lot like Christmas.
Russell sat there morosely nursing his ego, staring out, not down.
He was irritated.
The intercom buzzed once more.
He was ashamed.
Someone knocked. Russell completely ignored it.
He was feeling guilty.
The two shots of bourbon gave him a buzz. He was stoic and unbending.
A local high school chorus group began caroling in the square.
He was anxious.
As he watched, he brooded.

Eleven

"Make a right here, Greg, on Adams Street." Ray's glance switched back and forth from the blown up portion of the Harrisburg and environs map to the street signs in front of them. "And then take a left turn on North Second and then we'll go down and make a right onto Raspberry Alley towards Front Street." He acted it out in the air before his face with his finger. The two clerics negotiated their way in the Borough of Steelton less than one mile below the southern boundary of the City of Harrisburg. As long as both had lived in the region, neither had traveled down in these parts near the steel mill.

"Now we know why Duane showed up in this area, don't we," Greg remarked, slowly looking from side to side at the duplex houses badly in need of repairs on North Second Street. "But I wonder how Pam wound up here. Because I don't think she was originally from this locale, at least from what I can barely recall about her at China Beach. She was one of the nurses with the M.A.S.H unit. And I think I remember her being from North Carolina somewhere. Her last name was Means or something close to that"

A snowball whizzed past the windshield. Another hit the trunk of the car. Greg rode the brakes even more as their vehicle obviously was caught in the middle of a winter skirmish between the neighborhood kids. Precipitation from the night before dropped three inches of fresh snow on the ground, the best for making snowballs but the most dangerous because it was wet and heavy. Greg wanted out of the line of fire but did not want to risk hitting a rag-tag, snow-covered, young warrior running from between two parked cars. So he crawled along until it was time to roll onto Raspberry Alley.

"Maybe Ken's from here and the two hitched up when she got back to the States."

"Well, that's what Bill Learney surmised. That she came home from Vietnam and, after Robert was born, was visiting a friend here in Steelton where she met Ken at a local dive."

"I'll say this," Ray commented, "whoever this kid of his is, he sure could use a little help. Look at this neighborhood." They passed a number of houses with run-downed porches and steps that had yet to be shoveled, whose roofs and siding needed far more attention than clearing a recent snowfall.

Fr. Greg had received a follow-up call from Learney that Duane's son might be Robert Quoins, living with his mother in these parts and had asked the priest to check it out for the department, saving him a trip if it were a false lead. According to Bill, Ken Quoins had died three years ago from too many long backbreaking hours as a millwright, or more realistically from lung cancer caused by alcoholism and smoking. When he met Pam, her baby was about 16-months-old and the two eventually married. He took responsibility for Robert but never officially adopted him. Together they had four children of their own, all of which were still at home in the two-story row house on Raspberry.

Greg barely found a spot big enough to parallel park the

car. He took his time wedging between a beat-up 1979 Ford escort with a cracked window on the driver's side and a newer Dodge truck. Another sopping snowball slammed into the car door on his side as the first real battle of the winter season tumbled onto Raspberry. The two men gathered their gloves; Greg buttoned his overcoat leaving the roman collar visible; Ray reached into the back seat for his fur Daniel Boone-like cap.

"Hey, remind me on the way back to your car at the restaurant parking lot. I've gotten at least four more letters since I was up at the seminary. And I think I might know who it is."

"Are they as juicy as the others?"

"Absolutely. One more salacious than the other. This person could easily make a fortune writing adult books." Greg pulled the keys from the ignition and put them in his pants pocket. He reached for the door handle. "You know, at first they really bothered me because I thought I may have been inadvertently leading someone on. But I've come to realize it is just someone who needs help and I just happen to be the object of her sexual fantasies." He smirked factiously. "I guess I'm just a sex god even at this age."

Ray grinned as he pulled the inside flaps over his ears. "The curse, my man, the curse."

Five scrappy looking kids, each more wet and icy from the mêlée, 3 white kids and 2 blacks, surrounded the clerics as they started up the snow packed, dilapidated steps at 2473 Raspberry. The scrawny bunch, mostly 11 or 12 year-olds spotted their collars.

"What' cha preachers want here?" the skinniest one in the pack asked.

"We're looking for the Quoins." Greg answered.

"What fer?" one of the black kids fired back. "They don't go to church or nothin'."

"Ahhh, we just want to talk to Robert's Mom. Robert Quoins does live here, doesn't he?"

105

The motley troupe yipped in unison. "Yep!"

"But Robert can't talk to no strangers," the black kid piped again without prodding from any of the other four.

He was interrupted in his explanation by a sixth, slightly older teen running up the crumbled sidewalk from Front Street. The boy was taller than the rest, had a dirty, frayed and faded Philadelphia Eagles tousle cap pulled way down over his ears and almost shielding his eyes. He wore a multi-colored cloth jacket; a big rip up the right arm and a lot more tattered than the other kids' coats. He sloshed in the slush of ice and snow with two different sized boots; the top three buckles open on both of them.

"What' cha want at my house?"

"He lives here," the black kid barked again, "his name's Ken."

Greg and Ray respectfully addressed the new arrival, realizing he must be a junior. "We're looking for your Mom, Ken. I am Fr. Greg and this is Fr. Ray." He presumed the informal introductions would soften the discourse.

"She ain't home. She's working." The younger Ken had a suspicious look and seemed not at all impressed with the clerical titles. "What' cha need her fer?"

Greg countered with his own question to help begin an initial investigation. "And is your brother, Robert, therefore, watching all of you?"

The entire group erupted into guffaws and laughter, hooting and hollering, slapping their thighs and giving teasing high-fives with their frozen gloves. Greg and Ray were caught short with the seemingly ridicule of the query.

"Robby can't do nothin'!" Ken railed. "My sister Judy watches us while my mum works."

"Oh?"

"Yeah, my brother Robby's retarded. He can't do nothin'."

The band of ruffians initiated a singsong. "Retard! Retard!" pointing to each other as well as Kenny out of boyish, but destructive jest.

And Ken, himself readily joined the put down, pointing back at each of the crew. "Haaaa, you're all idiots like my brother, the big dumb retard."

The two priests cringed at the display of childish, uncharitable disrespect for each other and Greg sought to change the temper. "Can I ask you, Kenny, where your Mom works?"

"At the Laundromat," he gestured towards the mill, "on Front, around the bend. Yous can walk there if yoins want. My mum does. We don't have no car or nothin'."

"Where?"

"At old man Kriley's place. She works there every day. Gives change and shit to people wushing their clothes."

Greg decided he had what he needed from the boys and motioned Ray to go to the Laundromat by foot, leaving the car in the unprotected parking spot. Three other spaces along the alley had wooden kitchen chairs blocking them, thus saving them for the current occupant of the house in front of which they sat.

"Thanks, guys. Don't get too cold, playing." The hooligans scrutinized until both men turned the corner onto Front Street.

"Interesting." Ray remarked when they were out of sight.

"Yeah, to say the least. Sounds sad." Greg spotted the location as he tapped his compatriot on his shoulder. "Hey, thanks for coming with me, Corney. But what happened? I just realized that you were supposed to go down south this week."

"Oh, my brother-in-law won a sales contest and took my sister to San Francisco for three days this week. He won plane tickets to wherever he wanted to go." Ray waved his hands to dramatize the value of the prize. "I think I'm going down their place the end of next month. And that'll be just fine for me if the winter stays as fierce as it has been so far up here."

They reached Kriley's. Greg held the door for a tiny female patron carrying a larger than life basket of clean clothes to her car. There were four more regulars inside, three at the washers and one drying her clothes. All suspiciously turned to gawk when the priests entered.

"Looking for Pam Quoins," Greg said to the nearest lady standing at the second washer in a long line of white appliances, "can you tell me if she's here?"

The woman said nothing, just motioned to the small room in the back with the door wide open. Greg and Ray walked together like two fish out of water to the back of Kriley's.

"Pam?"

A hardened, very overweight attendant in her late forties, early fifties, an apron with many pockets, most of them filled with various coin denominations, strung around her large waist, stood up from her chore. She was gathering little boxes of soap power needed to refill the machines on the wall near the front of the Laundromat.

"Yeah? And who wants her?"

She displayed the same unfriendly and distrustful attitude as everyone they met on this exploratory excursion.

"I'm Fr. Greg Pugh," he extended his hand. The woman did not take it, mainly because she had her arms full of little detergent packages. "Sorry." Greg realized the absurdity of trying to shake her hand. "Maybe you remember me from Vietnam. I met you at the R & R center at My Khe when you were there with the M.A.S.H. corps."

"You mean China Beach?"

"Yeah."

Balancing the little boxes against her full-figured, drooping breasts, Pam Quoins leaned back and squinted up as Greg who was a head taller. "Yeah, I guess you look a little familiar. So, what 'cha want with me?"

"Can we talk somewhere?" He offered to carry some of her paraphernalia. She brushed past him.

"Yeah, come up front. Let me dump these by the dispenser." He settled for the plan knowing it was anything but a private meeting.

"It's about Duane Slubbler," Greg said as she sat her large frame on a wooden chair near the wall. It creaked with its overwhelming burden.

"Oh, what's the son-of-a-bitch up to now? Haven't seen him for a long time. Stopped helping with Robbie about a year ago." Pam elaborated, tossing her hands helter-skelter, "shows up out of the blue, helps a few years, and then disappears into thin air again like the first time!" She grabbed a pack of cigarettes out of one of the pouches of the apron and started to light a filtered one with a throw away lighter.

"He died."

"Really? What happened? One of them drug dealers finally pop him for pimping their territory?" Pam exhibited no sympathy whatsoever, turning her face slightly and letting out a stringy jet of smoke from the corner of her mouth.

"He shot himself. Suicide. The middle of November." Greg thought he needed a fuller explanation at the moment. "He was living at the retreat house where I live. Up above Harrisburg."

"Whoa." She looked down, shaking her head. "At least the son-of-a-bitch was good at something besides a good roll in the hay." The cynicism did not escape the two clerics. "Actually I take that back. When he surfaced here a few years ago, he was willing to put up some money for Robbie's keep." She shifted on the chair and the priests standing before her like school children thought the faulty piece of furniture might crack under the weight. "Came every week for a number of years with money … probably dope money … for Robbie. Helped a lot, especially when Ken croaked."

Pam sounded like she was delivering a belated, but crude eulogy. All shared a moment of silence, perhaps out

Jim Caldwell

of deference to Duane's memory. She drew a long drag on the cigarette and let it out. "But then the son-of-a-bitch disappears again ... faster than a varmint with a shotgun pointed up his ass ... just like he did when I told him I was knocked up with his kid."

"Duane lived his last year at our retreat house. He was sick with all kind of things, prostate cancer, diabetes, his nerves were shot. I guess it all got to him."

"Hell, he don't know what troubles are 'till he's lived in this dump a long as I have, no husband here to help, saddled with five mouths to feed, one of them special."

"Special?"

"Yeah, had a very bad time popping him out and his brain lacked enough oxygen."

"Robert?" The scene with the neighborhood kids suddenly made sense.

"You got it, preacher. Robbie ... the end result of Duane's wayward seed, his bastard son." She mellowed slightly, if you can call it that, as she sifted in her seat. The other patrons didn't mind the personal admissions, as they already knew the story. "Don't get me wrong. I love him dearly, but I'm burdened with him the rest of his life. The others will leave, but Robbie can never."

"We're here to put you in touch with the Department of Veterans Affairs. With Duane's death, Robbie might be entitled to some monetary and medical benefits."

"Really? Like what?" Another puff straight up into the air. "The army don't care about nobody. Besides I'm already on welfare."

"Not true. There is help for children of Vets up to a certain age and I think your son is still eligible and I think it might be in addition to your assistance, plus with Robert being ... Well, I don't know the particulars but I do have a name, address, and phone number of someone who might help. Name's Bill Learney. Came to me looking for Duane's son. I didn't even know he had a son, or that you were so close in the district. Somehow Learney got some information about you and asked us to look you up."

"I put Duane's name on the birth certificate even though he wanted to deny it at first. But it was his, all-right. Trust me." Pam's shoulders sagged as she looked away, perhaps remembering the early days. Her cigarette burned down to her fingers. One last drag and she stomped it out on the concrete floor of the Laundromat. "Sure was a handsome son-of-a-bitch in those days. And sexy as hell. What a lusty month of July we had at China Beach!" Pam prolonged the arousing memory trip. "What a great lover in bed. The man sure knew what to do alright even though he *was* a frick'n junkie."

Realizing she spoke erotically in front of two men of the cloth and came close to dropping the "F" bomb, Pam recoiled. "Oh, you know what I mean." But she continued despite the fact, justifying her past actions with waving gestures towards the two visitors. "Well what did you expect, hot young bodies in the prime of their sexuality, scared, lonely, at war with no one back home understanding nothin'. Foolin' around was bound to happen. It took your mind off the horrors of that stupid place for a moment or two."

"I just wish the son-of-a-bitch would have faced up to it then. Maybe we could have had a life together. But no, he denies the whole thing and runs ...didn't see nor hear from him 'till he shows up here five years ago. Shit, Robbie was already in his mid-teens." Pam shrugged. "Oh well, at least he helped for awhile. I guess I'm sorry he died." She looked at everyone there, the priests, the patrons, as though she was expecting them to clap for a great performance.

Neither priest moved, nor spoke.

"Hey you," she flapped up at Greg, "come to think of it, you know what I'm talking about. 'Member?" The paunchy, hard-boiled woman, crushing the wooden chair, stared directly up at him, pointing her pudgy finger. "You know, I 'member you for sure now that I've gotten a better look. I 'member you and that cute nurse from the OR ... what the hell was her name ... Julie something or other ...got pretty *chummy* if I recall." Pam cracked a sly grin and crossed her arms across her wide bosom. "*You two* spent a lot of time together ...on the beach ... that lusty month of July." She pounced on the word 'lusty' with no shame in stating for all in earshot what came next. "I'll bet you guys fought off the demons of your fears with lots 'a pleasures of the flesh." Pointing again, she dragged out the last declaration like a little kid snipping: "*Right?*"

Greg blushed like a railroad beacon. Ray knew the whole story, okay, but having it said again, out loud, caused great embarrassment to his friend standing there in a roman collar, a symbol of celibacy and self-restraint. Greg had duly confessed his sexual transgressions at the time, and rededicated himself to his vocation. It was all in the past. And few knew, except Ray, his confessor in the field, and of course, Julie. But now all the strangers in Kriley's Laundromat also knew.

Greg wanted to immediately run from the spot back to the car. Instead he changed the subject fast. "Can I give you the gentleman's name and information at the Department of Veterans' Affairs?"

"Shit, yeah!" Pam dug into the last pocket on her left side of the big apron and came out with a pencil and small pad. The top page was wrinkled and she ripped it off for Greg to have a clean one.

The priest carefully printed Bill Learney's name, address, and telephone number in Washington D.C. and handed it back. "He is very nice and courteous. I'm sure he will help you and Robbie in anyway possible. I'll call him when I get back tonight and tell him I found both of you."

Pam crushed the note back into the same pouch of the apron, raised her enormous body from the chair with great effort and proceeded to fill the soap dispensers. "Be cool, honey, and if you ever see that saucy lover of yours again, give her my best, if she 'members my name."

Greg pulled beside Ray's '85 Cavalier in the parking lot of Mama Leona's home town diner on North Harrisburg Street three miles over the city line. They had met earlier in the day for lunch.

"Thanks again, Corney, for going with me. I appreciate it. Sure didn't expect all that."

"Listen, you okay? With her mentioning Julie and all?"

"Oh, sure. I'm fine. Told you long ago, it was just simply a couple lonely and scared kids," he waved from where they had come, "as Pam said ... helping each other through some very dramatic times." He hesitated. "But I must admit. With us, I'd like to think it was more than that. When Bill first showed up, and I found some old China Beach pictures ... and ..."

Ray waited.

"I saw her picture for the first time in years, and I got that good feeling all warm inside that love can give." Greg held the steering wheel with both hands and twisted his head to speak honestly. "And you know, Ray. I think I've been a better priest because of her. I think I better understand peoples' feelings and trials of love and marriage. Know what I mean?"

Ray huffed a breathe of air. "Yes, I do, don't forget ... D.C."

"That's right." Greg's eyes followed a young couple putting grocery bags from the Shop Mart at the end of the strip-mall into the trunk of their car. "I remember reading this poem or essay or something on retreat a few years ago about special people coming in and out of our lives, ... leaving deep footprints on our hearts, footprints that change us forever to the good." The young husband kissed his wife as the two went to their respective car doors. "There was a great line about *treasuring the intersections* of such special meetings in case you never see them again ... " Greg turned back to Ray. "Well, we've both been better off knowing the love of a woman, haven't we?"

"Oh, I like that. Got to mark that down," Ray simulated writing on his left hand to lighten the mood. "Bet I use that in a homily before you do."

"Bet you will too, knowing you. You steal all my good ideas."

"Hey, but tell me more about the new letters. You said to remind you when we got back here."

"Oh, I don't want to get into that now. I have to get back and besides I'm not in the right frame of mind. Let's just say, I think I may know who it is. And I have a plan to confront her." He reached to turn the car heater down. "Come up for New Years, why don't you and we'll talk about it then. Come and eat."

"Probably can't do because it's a Sunday, but why don't *you* come down to the seminary the following Friday and concelebrate the feast of the Epiphany with us. Besides, Bede's been failing. I don't know what to tell you, but you may want to come down and see him soon."

"Got ya. That's a good idea. Take care, my brother."

Twelve

Bent over from age and arthritis, the tiny grandmother took hold of the bar and pulled herself up the two steps into the bus. Hunter sat in the aisle seat directly behind the driver. Immediately he jumped up as she struggled to reach the top. "Thank-you, honey," she said. Hunter nodded and headed towards the back of the crowed vehicle.

The terminal in Erie was inundated with travelers, all ages, trying to get to their destination for New Years Eve. Julie and the girls had driven Hunter over from home since he found the most direct bus route to Newark out of the Pennsylvania city. They would ride down route 79 to the turnpike and trek across the state.

Carrying the small blue and yellow Garrison U. duffle bag, Hunter stepped lightly with excited anticipation of seeing Alicia late that afternoon. Another aisle seat was empty in the next to the last row, catty corner to the bathroom. *Good move,* he laughed to himself, *will save me some steps during the trip.*

Jim Caldwell

An unshaven, longhaired, pony-tailed man in a black leather jacket, a silver chain from a pocket watch attached at the other end to his thick belt looping down his left thigh, slumped in the crevice between the seat and the side of the bus. He slept, arms crossed and his motorbike cap shielding his closed eyes, barely moving his stretched legs for anyone else to sit beside him comfortably. The sandy blond passenger wore tight buckskin pants and black boots blocking part of the aisle side. But Hunter didn't mind the inconvenience, feeling wound up inside that the day had finally arrived. Everyone jostled right and left in his or her place as the bus rolled onto 12th Street.

Grandma's petite, powder blue pillbox hat barely topped the back of her seat up front. She looked like a little dot so far away and reminded Hunter of his own grandmother, his Mom's Mom, who passed away when he was in tenth grade. Julie was from Warrenton, Virginia. And although, Hunter and his sisters rarely saw their grandma – she was in a nursing home at the end, her own husband having died when Julie was twelve - he felt a closeness to her because of his Mom. The grandparents on his Dad's side, however, never built much of a bond with the grandchildren. They were nice, but aloof.

Hunter couldn't contain his excitement. *Boy, I hope she likes it.* He unzipped the duffle on his lap and retrieved a green plastic shopping bag enveloping a prize of some sort. The character beside him shifted as he drooped lower against the corner of the window and repositioned his legs even more into Hunter's space. Again it was no bother. Hunter simply swung his own legs further into the aisle, turning his back to the seat partner.

Unraveling the bag, he couldn't resist one more peak. The rustling of the package made the shifty looking individual lift one eye then close it again. Hunter pealed the bag open enough to view the present he had for Alicia. He was tempted to take it completely from the confines of the container but reconsidered, preferring more to open the sack very wide and stare at the treasure.

A decent sized, white teddy bear with a large, red, half-heart piece of material with a jagged edge carefully embroidered on its fluffy, puffy belly, an innocent smile on its stuffed face, gazed back from the synthetic cave. Hunter had it personally created for Alicia by the mother of his sister Lonnie's friend who owns a novelty party store. Within the half-heart portion was an ornate, black 'H'. Feeling happy, he took hold of the real-life half-heart pendant and cross around his own neck through his sweatshirt.

But the most important part of the Christmas gift encircled the bear's neck on a gold chain, a friendship ring with Alicia's sapphire birthstone neatly positioned in a tiny heart. The piece of jewelry bounced up and down on the bear's padding with the rocking motion of the bus. In Hunter's estimation, the two of them had reached a new stage in their relationship. The starry-eyed collegian fiddled with the ring, picturing Alicia's face receiving it, and wondered if the gift would lead to an even deeper intensity. Right now his instinct said it was okay with him if that happened. *Mmmm, I love you.* Hunter pulled the bag close to his chest.

"Cute. Real cute."

The harsh, unsympathetic voice burst Hunter's romantic bubble. He quickly scrunched the bag with both hands.

"Be still my heart in the face of young love."

The Shakespearian-like declaration did not fit the unrefined appearance of the orator. Hunter twisted sharply to the dubious person beside him, still stretched across the whole space, arms still folded, but eyes wide open.

"Pardon me!"

"Don't get your shorts in a bunch, kid, I'm just jerking your chain," the man sneered, "no pun intended about the chain and all."

Hunter wasn't sure whether to respond or not. The bus

swayed back and forth traveling with good speed. Many of the passengers were reading something; some slept or had earphones in their ears with eyes closed. Few conversed, despite that it was already 10 in the morning. Hunter shrugged off the interloper's statements, preferring not to have a dialogue.

But the man persisted. "Girlfriend's?"

"What?"

"Is that for your girlfriend? Is that where you're goin' with that?" He jabbed his finger twice at the green bag.

"Yeah." Hunter was curt.

"Where?"

"Newark."

"Harrisburg for me."

"Okay." Hunter did not want to encourage him.

"To see my twelve-year-old." The man finally moved his legs closer to his own space allowing Hunter to also shift into his seat. He straightened and grabbed the back of the seat in front of them. "Excuse me, kid. Gotta piss."

Hunter stood again to let him back into his window seat. He had safely tucked Alicia's present back into the duffle and pushed it closer to his seat on the floor behind his feet. "You goin' home?"

"Used to be. Just visiting my daughter now. Been divorced for eight years."

Hunter's cheerful gut feelings were now tempered with the word, divorce, reminding him of his parent's troubles.

"Want to see her?"

"Sure."

The shaggy looking personality pulled a photo from the top pocket and pushed it before Hunter.

"You say she's twelve? She's very good looking for that age."

"You bet. Her mother always was. Now, my Brit's going to be thirteen next month. Yeah, a wild teenager."

"Was?"

"Was?" The man repeated Hunter's question back.

"Yeah, you said 'her mother *was.*' What's that mean? Did she die?"

"Oh, no," he huffed, "not quite that bad, but close. Well, it's like this, kid. She's still a good looker on the outside... but very ugly on the inside."

The negative philosophy pronounced without much prodding created a conflict within Hunter. It was a long jaunt ahead. Conversation would make it go faster. But he wasn't sure of his companion's attitude or what he might provoke.

Hunter likewise had to use the bathroom and got up.

"Where do you live now?" Hunter asked upon returning thinking a more positive approach would produce a better dialogue if they were to talk. He started to feel lethargic and sluggish although he had injected his insulin the first thing that morning. Quickly Hunter retrieved a candy bar from his coat pocket and gobbled it down in two quick bites.

The man looked sideways at the sudden hunger pang display. "Erie," he said with a knit brow, continuing to question the unduly intake of chocolate with his facial expression.

Hunter sensed the awkwardness. "Didn't have much breakfast this morning. How long have you lived there?"

"Since Brit's Mom and I split. Now she lives with her new lawyer husband and I'm remarried."

Hunter felt the pinch again with the term, lawyer. "Any more kids?"

"No. This one can't have them. So Brit comes with us a few weeks in the summer, and I go out there for a few days in the wintertime. My present wife just loves her. Maybe someday she'll come out here to live permanently."

Hunter sensed a softness under the rough façade.

"Regardless of her mother's thinking that she's so much better than me, I've always tried to be a good Dad." The man looked out the window at the turnpike entrance sign as he spoke, and not at Hunter. The bus came to a dead stop as the driver pulled the toll ticket from the machine.

I just met him, Hunter thought. They were only seat companions an hour and a half. *Should I share my anger about my parents' fighting?* He pressed his foot against the soft contents of the bag. At the moment he had mixed emotions. *It's a great opportunity. The man's a total stranger. I'll never see him again.* He could let out his frustrations. It might help.

"I admire you for that. And my Dad's been a good Dad ... but right now I am so damn pissed off at him!"

The macho man lifted his head off the window at the last sentence and extended his hand. "Tom ... Tom Sorbie."

"Hunter Harrisson," returning the handshake.

"Pissed off, huh?" The tough eccentric sounded a counselor's pitch out of the blue.

Hunter hesitated but relented from holding back.

"Damn him, my Mom's pregnant and he walked out on her! That pisses me off royally!"

"Pregnant? How old are you, kid?"

"21."

"Whoa. You'll be more of an uncle than a brother." He realized it was not funny. "How old is you Mom?"

"In her early forties."

"Ahhh," Tom slightly slapped his knee, pursing his lips. "A surprise bundle of joy late in life, huh?"

"I suppose."

"And your Dad's not ready to go through the diapers and being up nights with a crying newborn."

"Worse than that." Hunter felt a release to finally thrash out the situation with someone who didn't know him from Adam. "He claims the baby's not his. Says he had a vasectomy."

"Whoa, that's heavy, man." Now he appeared more like a buddy than a counselor as he questioned. "Is it true?"

"Is WHAT true?"

"Did he have a vasectomy?"

"I don't know! But I *do* know it's *his* baby. Who else's could it be?" Hunter was indignant. "My Mom's not like that! She would never be unfaithful!"

The burst struck Tom as he moved away from him and closer to the window.

"Didn't mean any harm, man. Just asking. 'Cause you seem so bent out of shape about the whole deal."

"I am!" Hunter put his head down into his chest. "I know they still love each other. I can recognize the signs now that I'm older and feeling the same things. So I just don't understand why my Dad's being such an ass about this whole thing? My Mom's so great and..."

"Hate to say it, man, but maybe he's got a little extra something goin' on? Those things do happen, you know. On both sides." Tom glared out the window again. The next words were not necessarily meant for his young friend's ears. "Everyone always presumes it's the man who strays, but women do too."

Hunter resented the inference about his Dad, or was he conjecturing it again about his Mom? At any rate, this time he kept his feelings to himself. He said nothing.

"How old is your Dad?"

"Upper forties. Believe me, he's always been a good father. 'Till this."

The man sitting beside him, a man who barely scrapped through high school, kept morphing into the psychologist. "We get tired, kid ... in a long-term commitment. It takes effort and thought everyday." This wise, straggly stranger had Hunter's full attention. "I'm sure your folks love each other, kid. It takes an awful lot to take that away." It was obvious he was still in love with his first wife, the mother of Brit. "But things happen when we get tired. We let our guard down. And things get goofy, until..."

Hunter faced the man, who had become the guru on top of the mountain, answering his inner questions. "Until what?"

"Until something dramatic happens, good or bad, that forces them back to their senses."

Hunter pondered his deep reflections.

"And you know things sometimes can be far, far better when they fight through this thing ... better than you could imagine." He had a regret in his voice. "God knows I tried immensely with Sue, but-- nothing happened like I'm telling you -- and she finally flaunted the fact that she never did love me and went to bed with someone she felt was as good as her and far above me," he said remorsefully. "We were pregnant before we married. Maybe she never did love me and just went along with it because of our daughter."

Hunter felt for him, bonded in sorrow with a total stranger and, in a way, it did relieve some of his angst. He was glad he opened up.

Tom put his hand on Hunter's shoulder in encouragement. "Hang in, there, kid. If they truly love each other, he'll be back." His grip felt strong and confident. "If your Dad's as good as you say, he'll come around. Maybe the baby's arrival will be the key. Maybe something else. Who knows?" He pushed Hunter slightly. "Just love them both in the meantime."

"Thanks." Hunter said, reaching to shake hands.

"You bet, kid." The two talked all the way to Harrisburg as though they had known each other for years. They chatted more about Tom's life, his daughter, Hunter's college life, Alicia and how he was going to spend New Years with her family. The bus pulled into the Post House Cafeteria as the conversation between these two passing ships wound down.

"We will have a 40 minute layover at this Harrisburg terminal," the driver announced from the center of the aisle. "Those debarking here, we thank you for traveling with the Smolly Bus lines. Those of you proceeding on to points east, with our final destination being Newark, New Jersey, please secure your seats so new passengers know they are taken, and *please* do not leave anything of value in the bus if you get off to grab somethin' to eat."

Hunter was starved. The candy bar helped but he needed more. Snatching the duffle, he waited impatiently to leave the bus. Grandma remained seated. Hunter made it a point to smile at her.

The holiday mob was enormous. *Hell of a lot of people going somewhere on News Years Eve.* He marched straight to the concession stand hanging the bag onto his arm and reaching to pull a couple of dollars from his wallet. Three lines formed within minutes. Hunter tagged the end of the third column nearest him and waited his turn.

Aimlessly checking the billboard above the counter, he settled on the usual all-American lunch of burgers, fries and a cola, not the best diet for a diabetic but what choice did he have. People excused themselves breaking the row to pass through. Hunter stepped back and moved forward more than once in the line to order.

Finally.

Round tables, chest high, stood like sentinels a few yards away in the food court. Spilled mustard, ketchup and used napkins cluttered most of them. Hunter spotted a relatively clean one and aimed at it, balancing the cardboard square with two cheeseburgers and an extra large sleeve of fries. They were falling over the top into the square and onto the floor. It distracted Hunter, head down, as he clung to the giant cola.

BAM!

Hunter lurched from the collision. More fries flew in all directions. The hefty beverage and ice splattered everywhere within a three foot circumference. Folks in the area scattered and grimaced at Hunter as though it were his fault someone bumped into him. The tall gentleman in the long black overcoat gripped Hunter from behind with both hands on his shoulders.

"Oh, I'm so sorry, young man." He pulled Hunter back from the mess. "Stay here. Let me get someone to clean this up and get you another drink." Everything happened so fast

"What the hell–"

The man rushed to the counter before Hunter could finish his complaint. He returned almost instantly with a new soda. Hunter had moved to the closest unclean table and set the box down, tossing the empty paper cup he retrieved from the floor into the trash container a few feet away. Someone already arrived on the scene to mop the wet floor as folks rushing here and there walked around the clutter in a wide circle.

"Here you are." The man set the substitute cold drink on the table. "I apologize again. I wasn't paying attention to where I was going."

"Yeah, that was a pretty damn stupid thing to--" Brushing the liquid from his pants, Hunter lifted his head spotting the collar. He was embarrassed.

"Aaah, thanks, Father."

The priest dashed on his way, looking up at the arrival board.

An older white haired gentleman walked though the door at the back of the terminal carrying a small, black travel case. He approached Hunter's unintended offender. "Thanks for picking me up with little notice, Greg."

"You're most welcome, Provincial, but I thought you weren't visiting us until the second week."

"That will be the official visitation. I was in Washington D.C. and just though I come spend News Years with you at the retreat house."

"You are always welcome, Father. Here let me take your bag."

The pair walked through the double glass doors in the front of the Post House unwittingly walking past Hunter as he re-boarded his bus for Newark.

Thirteen

Alicia caught sight of him through the windows moving from the back of the bus. Anxiously she dashed outside, leaving her parents and little brother standing inside the terminal. Hunter grinned broadly seeing her rushing to greet him. Her bounding the way she did reminded him of the current commercial on TV where two lovers bounce towards each other in a field of flowers and then at the last minute bump into each other and fall in laughter. There was giddiness in the present scene. But the other passengers would not debark fast enough. Hunter reached the front just as Grandma rose from her seat since she waited for the aisle to clear. As anxious as he was to leap down and ardently hug his Alicia, Hunter let grandma go first. It was a gentleman's gesture, characteristic of him, but heightening his impatience.

"Ohhhh, I missed you." She smothered him with a kiss and a strong embrace pressing her head sideways into his jacket. They didn't care where they were. They saw only each other. "And I especially missed this!" Alicia drilled his dimple with her finger, and rubbed his hair as though they were alone back at school. Eventually she took his hand with both of hers and pulled him towards the building. "Come on, my folks are waiting."

"So this is Newark," Hunter said as he tugged back waiting for the driver to pull his gear from underneath.

"Ohhhh, I'm so glad you came." Alicia pulled, then crushed into him for another hug, and then pulled again. Mr. and Mrs. Collier approached from the building.

"Hi, Hunter. Glad you could come and spend some time with us." Mrs. Collier kissed him lightly on the cheek.

Her Dad offered his hand. "Nice to meet you again, young man."

"And this is my annoying little brother, Brian."

A red-haired, 14-year-old with a punk haircut, a few pimples from acne among his freckles, wearing a hooded coat and jeans with a hole below the right knee waved his hand.

"Hey, dude."

Hunter almost blew it. He reached with an open hand, only to be met by the adolescent's hooked fingers waiting for him to hook on and pull instead of shaking the conventional way. At the last second, Hunter redeemed himself, hooking, yanking, opening and sliding hands. "Hey, dude." He sought to ingratiate himself immediately with the younger sibling. "You know my best friend in the world is also Brian. We're roommates at college."

"I thought my sister was your *best* friend." It was a unique observation for a teen in the early stages of puberty.

"She sure is," Hunter reached for Alicia hand, "but I mean he's my best *male* friend."

"Enough, Brian. We have to get going," Mrs. Collier said. "We have to get something to eat, get you to Aunt Sarah's, and get ready for the party." Alicia's Dad reached for the piece of luggage.

"That's okay, sir, but I'm good with it." Hunter said lifting the small bag from the pavement.

Brian turned up his nose. "Yeah, sure I spend New Year's Eve with the cousins while you guys get bombed and kiss it up."

"Oh, Brian," his Mom remarked attempting to muss his hair as her son ducked away.

Now it was Jodie Foster's eyes that followed Hunter around the room as he unpacked a few items from the case. The poster was life size, displaying the beautiful young actress in quite an aggressive pose as the female lead for *The Accused*. Alicia's Mom had determined that Hunter would occupy Brian's room and could lay clothes on top on the dresser if he wanted to rather than "live out of the suitcase." She specifically asked him to check to see if he needed a shirt or anything ironed for the party. Brian would sleep on the couch in the family room for the duration of his visit.

Hunter timidly protested saying he did not want to be such a bother but Mrs. Collier would not hear it. Perhaps it was her way of assuring that he and Alicia would not be together during the night. All the bedrooms were on the second floor and her parents slept with their door partially open. If he were in the family room, they could not be seen. *Mmmmm.* Hunter mused to himself*, was that on her mind or was she just being super hospitable?* But she didn't know him very well. Despite Hunter's desire to be with Alicia, he was honorable and would respect her parents' home.

Someone knocked. "Merry Christmas," Alicia sang, revealing a large wrapped present from behind her back. Surrendering it she offered a long, warm, sensuous kiss to accompany it. Hunter returned the favor mashing the cardboard box between them, and lifting her off the floor in the process. Nancy Collier couldn't patrol everything. "I really hope you like it."

The two sat on the edge of Brian's bunk. The NCAA basketball comforter on the bed appeared inappropriate for a romantic exchange of holiday gifts. Hunter slowly unwrapped, pushing his shoulder up against Alicia all the time, more enthralled with being beside her than what might be in the mangled package.

"Oh, I do like it." Hunter held up the bright red and white turtleneck sweater and studied the pattern of snowflakes speckled all over it. There were a corresponding tousle cap and scarf.

"You can wear them when we go skiing this Thursday." Alicia squeezed his arm. "It's a medium. Right?"

"Yeah." Hunter kissed her on the neck. "Thanks, 'Lic. I really like it. I've always like turtlenecks." It was time to tease. "Too bad, I forgot to get you something." Her boyfriend feigned regret and sheer embarrassment, lowering his head and shielding his eyes.

Alicia punched him. "You better have!" Hunter grabbed her hand, as she was about to punch a second time and the two rolled back onto Brian's NCAA matching pillow. Hunter faced her and stroked her long hair. "I love you so much. Thanks for inviting me."

Alicia kept the pressure on him. "Thanks nothin'. Where's my present?" She made him stand as she rummaged through his belongings pushing his underwear aside. "Come on, where is it? Is it big or small?" Hunter loved watching how playful she was, hoping it would stay like this the whole visit and not get moody like it did before Christmas. Alicia threw up her hands in jovial desperation. "I'm serious!'

"Okay, okay, I give up." Hunter had his own hands in the air like a bank robber had held him up. Backing towards the dresser he reached down for the duffle bag on the floor in front of it. Alicia followed closely. "You're like a wild banshee. I better come up with something ... to save my life." Another quick peck on the lips for kicks before the grand presentation.

Hunter handed her the plastic shopping bag.

"Mmmm. An Irish kid that does polish Christmas wrapping. Love it." The young couple giggled.

Alicia eyed the bear like a three-year-old rapidly understanding what Christmas presents are suppose to mean. She clutched it, hugged it and rubbed her cheek against it. With tears, she retrieved the friendship ring from the bear's neck and said everything with her moist eyes. Hunter unclipped the chain, slid the ring off of it and onto her finger.

"I love you." She whimpered like a puppy dog, burrowing into his chest and resting awhile in silence. Hunter did not see the worry in her eyes as she leaned against him. He only felt her warmth and smelled the freshness of her hair. He never wanted to let go.

"Thank you." Alicia whispered.

They held each other for a long time. And for a brief instance, Hunter intuited in his girlfriend that unexplained dithering between intimacy and distance. Her mother's voice broke the mood. "Hurry, guys, we're going to Molly's restaurant and it'll be crowded." They kissed long and hard before joining the family in the driveway.

"So, Hunter, Alicia tells us that your Mom is having a baby." Mrs. Collier followed right behind him at the salad bar, reaching across in front of him for croutons.

"Yes, she is," Hunter answered proudly at the same time catching the ashen, self-conscious look on Alicia's face on the other side over the glass hood, "she's due the first week in June. And I just think it's great. I can't wait." Looking across, he knotted his brow and raised his cheeks as if to say, *what's a matter?* Alicia looked away.

Brian squeezed against the wall in the booth next to his Mom and opposite Hunter and Alicia. He delved into his platter with little manners, dripping the juice from the tomato on his hamburger down his chin.

"You're a senior, right?"

"Yes, sir," Hunter responded to Alicia's Dad.

"So I suppose your university will have some fine civil engineering companies for you to interview with this semester?"

It was a question totally unexpected. Hunter stared not knowing whether Mr. Collier was joking or not.

"I'm—"

Alicia just about trampled his right foot with her heel.

"I'm — ouch!" He recovered. "Excuse me, I...I bit my tongue." All expressed amusement. Alicia's hand secretly whacked his leg under the table. "I would imagine they will."

He decided to enhance things, feeling it was somehow a gag. "Actually I'm more mechanical engineering. But I'll know more when the new semester begins in a couple weeks. I know from past years they have invited some big name companies to interview on campus."

But her Dad was serious! Hunter thought. *Alicia told them that and not that he was in music and the arts ... that he wanted to be in the theater?* There was the mystery again.

"Excellent. What does your father do?"

"He's a lawyer."

"Good. Any other brothers or sisters other than the expected one?"

"Oh, Harold, enough shop talk. The young man isn't one of the students at your high school." Nancy Collier tapped Hunter's arm across the table. "Good luck, whatever happens." She twisted to Brian. "Come on, now. Don't dally with your food. I would like to have an hour's nap before we head to Sarah's with you and then to the club."

Hunter felt the nervousness of Alicia beside him. The ambiguity reared its ugly head once more. At the moment he could not look at her.

The centerpieces for the tables at the Spring Garden

Country Club were large bouquets of freshly cut flowers, each with its own silver 1989 Happy New Year banner diagonally strapped across it. Champagne glasses graced each place at the huge circular table also with the imminent year embossed in gold numbering and waiting to toast the midnight hour. Alicia and Hunter's place cards sat directly across from her folks at the reserved Collier table.

As a long time member of the club Harold invited a number of friends and teachers from the school. "So, that's something about that Pan-Am flight exploding over Lockerbie," he said as he handed Bob Rickets a fresh beer, "might have been a couple of local kids on that thing."

"Oh, Harold, stop talking about news at a party," his wife interjected again, "leave the bad news 'till tomorrow. It will still be there as always."

"Well," her husband retorted to Bob, "I suppose it would be a lot more fun talking about Jimmy Swaggart getting defrocked over his sexual liaisons with women other than his wife." He smirked. "Did you see that dramatic crying jag for an apology on TV?"

Hunter came back from the bar with his second beer. Mr. Collier eyed him with a cocked eyebrow even though he witnessed Hunter being carded by the bartender. Alicia reacted unfavorably to the possible disapproving look, smacking her lips and furrowing her brow. However Hunter failed to notice it. Instead, he misread Alicia's creased continence and whispered. "Hey, what was that all about?"

"What was what all about?"

"At Molly's. The civil engineering bit. Did you really tell your folks that I was an engineering major?"

Alicia sheepishly nodded yes over top her ginger ale.

"Why?" The unknown side of her personality was challenging. It baffled Hunter.

"Cause."

"Cause why?"

Alicia turned her head away from the group, cupping her

mouth with her hand so her Dad would not be in earshot. "Because my Dad is so big on science." She frowned. "Why do you think I'm in Biology?" The frown deepened. "Not my choice."

"But…"

"But nothing." Alicia gave a childlike look of explanation. "I know it's not the truth. But I wanted both of them to like you off the bat." She lowered her head and peeked at him. "I'll tell them the truth after the skiing trip." She put her hand on top of Hunter's resting on the edge of the chair. "My Dad's been a high school counselor for years. His whole life is getting kids in college for a long-term career. It isn't that he doesn't like liberal arts, but … he just doesn't think it offers security … the theater and all." Alicia shrugged her shoulders at him as though this justified all. Hunter still felt uneasy, but the beer made it feel as if it wasn't the initial big deal he thought.

"Let's dance."

"Okay."

Alicia raced him to the wooden floor in front of the stage. Johnny and the Moonlights played everything from oldies of the 50's, 60's and 70's to rock and polkas. Hunter and Alicia lost themselves in the music and fun. They paused only to refill his beer.

"Ladies and gentlemen," the announcer interrupted a Johnny Mathis romantic cheek-to-cheek song, "it is countdown time. Just 15 minutes to the New Year. Those of you wishing to toast, return to the tables as the waiters fill your champagne glasses." People scurried off the floor in all directions.

The Collier party gathered in a circle raising their glasses in gleeful anticipation.

"Nine … eight … seven …the crowd launched into shouting the numbers with the emcee … three … two … HAPPY NEW YEAR!"

Auld lang syne burst from the band. Glasses pinged

against each other. People screamed out the familiar phrase. Horns tooted as streamers fell. Party favors unrolled with breath and held rigid until released.

Hunter grabbed Alicia for a passionate kiss that would take them from one year into the next. "This is *our* year, 'Lic!" Hunter shouted into her ear, kissing her lobe, her neck, kissing her again and again. "I can feel it in here," as he pounded his heart with his fist.

Alicia countered with equal exuberance. But she kept her face hidden, shielding a falling tear and an apprehensive expression. Everyone started grabbing each other for the new years' greeting. Mrs. Collier, her friends, ladies Hunter never saw in his life planted smackers on his face. Harold and his male friends offered the same to Alicia and all surrounding females. It was a free-for-all when finally the two came back around to each other. Alicia was completely crying, wiping both eyes with a bent index finger.

"You okay?"

Alicia hugged him tightly and spoke next to his right ear. "I'm late."

The beer had full effect along with the noise, the music and the frivolity. "Late for what?"

Alicia eyeballed him up close, distinctly pronouncing the words. "I'm late."

But the celebratory din of the room masked all seriousness. It escaped him as another one of Mrs. Collier friends snatched Hunter away and collared him for a kiss.

Fourteen

Elena's eyes tracked her travel case around the circular conveyor at Hopkins Airport at the same time glancing at her watch and looking in all directions. *I'm pretty sure I gave the right time of my arrival.* She examined the ticket stub in her hand. *Arriving Tuesday January 3rd, 3:45 P.M.* A husky gentleman in a tweed sports coat with leather patches on the elbows bumped her while retrieving his own baggage.

"Sorry."

"No problem."

But there was. Neither Julie nor anyone was there to meet her. *Must be tied up in traffic. I'll sit awhile and wait.*

Climbing into a taxi 50 minutes later, Elena rattled off to the driver the address ripped from Julie last letter. Surely there had been a miscommunication because the note in her hand specifically said that she and the girls would be at the airport in time.

Elena needed this break. Despite the tension in the house with Russell gone, she knew it would be relaxing to spend time with Julie and her family. She looked forward to it since before Christmas, even buying a new pants suit for the trip like a kid in anticipation of a school picnic. The plane ride from London was long and boring. The large framed passenger seated on her right near the window snored in her ear during the whole flight. Elena sighed as the cab driver pulled in front of the house, not seeing Julie's car. *Oh, no they did go for me and now I've messed things up for sure.*

No one answered the doorbell. She tried the door. It was unlocked.

"Hello," Elena sang cautiously walking from room to room. "Anybody home?"

The note in Julie's handwriting was pinned down under a saltshaker on the kitchen table: *At the hospital ... United General ... eastside of Cleveland.* For a renowned doctor usually composed with emergencies, Elena became tense and distraught. This was different. Julie was not a patient. She was a good friend whose pregnancy Elena had followed closely over the phone the past month and a half.

"United General, Cleveland."

"Lady I just dropped you off here ten minutes ago."

"I know."

"Emergency?"

"Don't know but I would appreciate getting there as fast as possible without breaking any speed limits." He did.

The older woman, fidgeting with the cord from the phone headset, looked over the wire-rimmed glasses perched near the tip of her nose. "Room 619 west. Elevators are around the corner. Go left when you get off on the sixth floor"

Linda Murasko was standing there when the elevator door slid open. Elena back stepped as the doctor joined her in the car. They were alone. They could talk professionally as Linda hit the button for the mezzanine where her hospital office was. Elena rode along.

"Linda!" Elena reached for both her hands and

squeezed. "What's up?"

"Sonogram showed an early case of placenta previa."

"Ohhhh, marginal or what?"

"No, a little more, blocking the cervix a quarter inch or so."

"Mmmm. So what are you thinking?"

"We should be okay if I can convince her to rest a lot and stay in bed the next few weeks." The two associates shared their concern for Julie. "I'm glad you're here, Elena. Maybe you can help persuade her to start her maternity leave from this place as of today."

Elena nodded. Linda shrugged, laying her stethoscope on the desk. "Even with her full cooperation, we may be facing a Caesarian. The fetus is in a slight transverse position. Of course, I should be able to turn the baby back into place, but I think I'll wait a few days until she's rested."

"Was she bleeding a lot ... a little?"

"No, just spotting, but with her age she was wise to call immediately. Maybe you can explain the situation a little more to the kids so they understand that we *do* have a concern but things should be okay if we keep on top of it."

"Sure, I'm here for a couple weeks so I can help."

"Is the husband helping financially these days? I know he's not living there."

"Don't know."

"Has she been talking to him?"

"Don't know that either. I try to wait for her to bring it up. Why?"

"Because it'd be beneficial for Julie to have as little stress as possible in the days and weeks to come. And if talking with him causes..."

"Understand. I'll nicely convey that to her when we get back to her place." Elena loosened up. "Boy or girl?"

"Julie wants to be surprised, soooo ....," Linda zipped her lips, "I'll never tell."

Elena embraced her. "Party pooper." She held both her

hands. "Gee, I'm thankful I found you for Julie. You're the best." They hugged again.

"I think I would like her to stay the night and go home tomorrow. That way, I can also check her blood pressure again in the morning. The baby's progress is looking fine."

"Okay."

As with most hospitals these days, the room was brightly decorated. Around the top of the walls near the ceiling ran a paper border of spring flowers. Julie sat propped up on two large pillows, her legs stretched under a light sheet and white spread, and sipping some water. Lonnie was on the far side of the bed holding her hand. Lynn was hovering over the food tray on the swing table asking if she could have the chocolate cake if Julie did not want it. Personnel from the tenth floor where Julie worked as the day nurse supervisor paraded in and out to wish her well.

"Oh, Elena, I am soooo sorry. But things happened so fast. We had no way to get a hold of you. You were already in the air."

Elena leaned down to kiss Julie as Lynn moved out of the way carrying the dessert to the chair near the window. "I'll forgive you ... this time." She straightened her glasses. "I found the note right away."

Lonnie seemed the most concerned. "So, guys tell me more. What is goin' on? Elena, are my Mom and the baby okay?"

"Honey, this is something that's commonly happens after a woman's had twins or triplets... especially if the mother is *older* at the time." She tossed a bogus look at Julie seeking to ease the young inquisitor with her casual and playful tone.

Julie laughed as she tapped Elena teasingly on the arm. "Hey, hey watch the *older* bit. May I remind you that we *are* contemporaries."

Lonnie still had no clear answer.

"It's a condition where the placenta, which is usually up

in the top part of the uterus," Elena was using both hands in the air to simulated the situation, "sometimes moves down the side and might block the cervix through which the baby is born." Lonnie followed her hands as they moved down the imaginary womb. It helped to explain. "If it blocks the opening too much, there can be complications as we get closer to birth."

"But what's does that mean? Will the baby be okay?" Lonnie fretted. "And what about my Mom?" The repetition of the questions from before showed that she did not fully understand Elena's explanation at the present time.

Julie was peaceful through the whole discourse, gratified by her daughter's loving concern.

"She's fine, hon.," Elena walked around the bed towards her, "and the baby should be fine." She moved to lighten things. "Your little brother or sister is growing and gettin' bigger ... anxious to meet his or her big sister." she tapped Lonnie square on the nose, "who will help take care of him or her. Right?" The teenager nodded, feeling relieved.

Elena addressed Julie. "When did things happen?"

"As we were leaving to get you at the airport. I started spotting a little. We waited as long as possible but it wouldn't stop. So I called Linda and met her here." She took Elena's hand. "Sorry for standing you up and causing such consternation."

"Ohhhh." Elena teased, "I suppose I'll get over it."

"So what do we have to do?" Lonnie questioned again.

"Well," Elena answered with a big grin, "you, your sister and brother, when he's home, have to help a lot more around the house ... cleaning and all. Because your Mom has to rest a lot ... take many, many naps and just sit in bed with her legs stretched out reading, watching TV or dozing or whatever. But she's not to strain herself in any way."

Elena spun in place pointing to each of the twins. "And you guys are not to get her riled up by talking back or being stubborn. Understand?"

"Yeah, yeah," they murmured in unison.

"It's not me, it's her," chanted Lynn, tossing her head towards Lonnie. But it was done in recognizable jest and so everyone chuckled.

The next statement went to Julie. "And you'll have more frequent visits with Linda. Obviously if you start bleeding again, call, as you did, right away. And I'm sure she told you that the baby is starting to breech."

"Yes. She said she'll turn him," Julie waved both hands on either side of her shaking head, "or *her* in a few days."

Lonnie wanted more answers.

"Will the cord thingy move back up?"

"Well, yes and no. It doesn't actually move by itself, but as the fetus grows and the uterus expands, it seems like the placenta moves back up away from the opening. In reality it doesn't actually move so much as the cervix opening moves away from it blocking it. Okay?"

Lonnie shook her head yes as though she comprehended the whole picture. She did not. However, Elena's willingness to explain everything lessoned her anxiety as well as the composed smile Lonnie saw on her Mom's face.

Lynn finished the cake, placing the empty plate on the tray. "Oh, man, I'm still hungry." Again everyone in the room laughed.

"Well, in that case, it's time to get out of here and let your Mom get some sleep." Elena grabbed both adolescents' hands. "Come on, guys, my treat. We're going out on the town for a good meal and maybe a movie."

All three kissed Julie.

"We'll be here around 10:00 tomorrow. Don't worry about a thing tonight. The girls and I are going to have a wild all-night party *without you*," she joked tilting her head to Julie, "and paint our toe nails, and gorge ourselves and gossip about boys and..."

It was music to Lonnie's ears.

Jim Caldwell

Aston Inn was as quaint and as beautiful as ever, and quite full to capacity for a Tuesday night. "Your Mom brought me here in November. I just love this place."

The twins looked around. Neither had ever been here. Lonnie spied Darlene moving quickly towards them in her quaint uniform.

"Hey."

"Thought your Dad wouldn't let you work on weekdays?"

"Yeah, but they called 'cause it's so busy. He said okay for tonight." Darlene broke away. "What are you guys doing here?"

"This is my Mom's friend," Lonnie pointed, "Elena. She's from England. My Mom's in the hospital and she's visiting."

Darlene barely reacted to the 'hospital' word. "Yeah, I remember seeing you with Mrs. Harrisson." She hustled away, signaling to the girls. "Later."

With no reservations, the three did not obtain a window table, yet even from the middle of the dining room, the red blinking lights on the buoys bobbing up and down created an aura like being on an island.

"This place is neat."

"Yeah, my Mom always promises that we'll come to the shops but haven't made it yet."

"But I think she and my Dad spent a weekend here last fall."

The twins jabbered. Elena loved it. She missed having teens of her own. Without wishing Julie any harm, she coveted having the girls to herself for an evening. Her own hassles faded away.

"I wanted to call Hunter, but Mom said not to bother him since things seem to be okay. She'll explain when he gets home."

"Yeah, and I wanted to call Dad, but Mom wouldn't let me. Said she wanted to talk to him."

Elena mentally noted the last words.

Their own charmingly dressed waitress handed each of

them an elaborate tri-fold menu.

"Anything you want, kids. Splurge ... on me."

"I don't recognize some of these things," Lonnie said.

Elena laughed to herself. "I can help."

"Es ... car ... *got*?"

Elena laughed again. "The 't' is silent. Escargooo..."

"Whatever. What is it?"

"I don't think you want that, honey."

"Why? What is it?"

Elena wrinkled her nose, put her hand to her mouth and whispered. "Snails. It's a French delicacy."

"Oh, my God." Lonnie shuddered. "Don't they have anything American like spaghetti or something?"

Elena loved it. Lynn threw her eyes to the ceiling and sighed. The night was fun. "They have a nice ravioli dinner, if you like Italian, Lonnie."

"Okay, that's what I'll have," thankful to find something she considered normal.

Suddenly Elena's smile morphed into a puckered brow when she saw them enter and be escorted to their table near the far corner window. The twins did not see him as their backs were to the lobby, nor did he catch sight of them.

Russell was having dinner with Christine.

Instinctively, Elena slouched down behind the menu. *Oh, my God.* She echoed Lonnie's phrase in her head but for a far different reason. They were about to order. Could they have their dinner without the girls seeing him? Should she approach him about Julie? The fun evening abruptly reversed itself. "I think I'll have the Prime Rib," she mumbled, closing her menu.

"And you've just *got* to meet him. He works in the kitchen here and he's just the cutest and..." Darlene had left her post for a few minutes to regal the twins with her latest infatuation, a young freshman working his way through the local community college. "He's from Warren and shares an apartment with a couple guys here in Mentor."

The girls were engrossed; Elena was disturbed. "Excuse me, girls. I have to go to the rest room." Hopefully Darlene could distract them long enough until she returned.

It really wasn't any of Elena's business with whom Russell was dining, but on the other hand, she has been unintentionally pulled into this situation. Her objective was to finish their meal and leave without his daughters seeing him with another woman. The thought of it drudged up her past failed marriage. She lost her appetite and desire to stay. Maybe freshening her face at the sink would help.

Christine stood beside her in the mirror touching up her own make-up. The distasteful shock of coming face-to-face with the woman who might be the cause of her good friend's marriage breaking up only deepened the ugly memories of the past. Elena lost control.

"You should be ashamed of yourself!"

The woman was incensed. "I beg you pardon. You talking to me?"

"Russell Harrisson. The man you're with. He's married, you know, and his pregnant wife is currently in the hospital with complications."

"I don't think *whom I'm with* is *any* of your business." Christine bristled. "So who the hell are you?"

"You're nothing but a slut!" The words even stunned Elena coming so uninhibited as they did. If the scene were a high school girls' bathroom instead of a plush powder room of a fine restaurant, the terse expressions may have caused a physical fight. Two other patrons anxiously witnessing the exchange quickly exited. Elena left in a flurry.

Christine did not follow.

"Let's have the baked Alaska, Elena. Is that okay? I've always wanted to have that." Lonnie pointed to the fake looking sample on the waiter's serving dish. "Isn't that the thingy that they set on fire?"

Elena was mixed. At the moment she wanted to flee the

Inn. At the same time, she did not want to alert the twins to the fact that their father was in the same room with, perhaps, his mistress. If she suddenly ended the dinner, Lonnie and Lynn would wonder. But she had said something stupid to Christine. *What if Russell came to the table upon hearing? No, he would not do that with her sitting there with his two daughters, would he?*

"That's for two people," Elena said as she furtively looked to see if Christine were relaying the episode to Russell, "so you both have to have it."

"Ouuuu, yeah. I'd love that." Lynn chimed.

The cart always attracts attention. Even the most sophisticated diner is fascinated with flaming baked Alaska. The servers at Aston's knew they had an audience and dramatized the lighting with flare. The girls looked like seven-year-olds on the fourth of July. Elena feigned delight with the scene as she kept a close eye on the table with Julie's husband.

Russell slapped a five-dollar tip down on the table in a huff as the two rose to leave. It appeared they were heading in their direction. Elena braced herself for a humiliating confrontation. The couple turned hurriedly and left, both throwing daggered looks in her direction.

The twins saw nothing but the flaming dessert.

Fifteen

"I have so many sleepless nights, especially these days, wishing you were lying in my bed beside me..." Greg studied the latest letter from the unknown admirer. "...I just want to stroke your face ..." The priest wasn't disturbed anymore, just concerned and forming a plan to help. "I want to feel the full length of your tall muscular body touching mine..."

Something struck him as he read. Opening the bottom drawer, Greg retrieved the small bundle of letters, six in all counting the one lying on the desk. One by one he examined them. *Mmmmm, this is interesting.* He was right with what caught his attention.

"Father." Karen knocked on the office door. Greg quickly covered the letters including the current one with the opened dictionary he had been using to check a word for the newsletter.

"Yes?"

"I need to ask a big favor."

"Yes, Karen."

"I know things are very busy, with the planning committee meeting twice this week and all, and with next week being the visit of your ... what is he called again?"

"The Provincial. Our local community is part of a number of places that made up what we call a Province."

"Well, with you being tied up with that and all, I was wondering if I could take Thursday and Friday off this week?"

"Ohhhh?"

"There's a concert down in DC and one of my friends from college invited a bunch of us down to stay overnight Thursday at her place for the concert and spend Friday in Washington ... shopping."

"Sounds like an expensive adventure."

Karen wasn't amused.

However, Greg recognized a good possibility. "Do you think your Mom would be able to help fill in? I know she's here for tonight's meeting and again Thursday night, but if she could come in a few hours that afternoon, I would appreciate it." He elaborated about how opportune it could be. "In fact, it could work out great since she could run off the list from tonight for the second meeting Thursday night."

"I don't think she would mind. Let me call her right away."

"Good. I'll really only need her a few hours on Thursday and, of course for the meeting. I was going to take off Friday myself. It's the feast of the Epiphany and I'm goin' down to the seminary in York to visit."

Karen reached her desk when her boss called her back. "By the way, did you get typed what I asked?"

"I did it at home last night."

This is uncanny, Greg thought. The plan was unfolding itself with little effort. *I can compare.* "Thank you so much. I am so crammed these days."

The young secretary handed him the three pages. "I hope this is okay. Our typewriter at home really needs a new ribbon. I keep reminding my Mom to buy one."

"That's fine, Karen. I just needed a draft copy from the dictate machine." He smiled at her. "Thanks again for everything." Karen moved to leave. "Hey, whose concert is it?"

"Pat Benatar."

"Who?"

Karen giggled as his not being familiar with the popular singer. "Pat Benatar. She's a hard rock singer. Nothing you would like." Both knew there was a musical generation gap.

Greg held the draft copy of the talk in his left hand, the latest letter in his right. *Mmmmm the 't's' and the filled in 'o's'.* He reread the new letter. It hit him a second time. Laying it down, he circled the repeated word. Checking the other offerings once more, Greg was convinced that it only showed up in this one. *Mmmmm.*

"Fr. Tim," Greg addressed him from the podium, "did you and your committee get us a good line up for the Lenten series?"

The room had three full tables of participants. In his role as Director, Greg stood in the center before the entire group. A large green movable board stood behind him, an agenda written in ABC bullet points.

"I think we have some good possibilities." Tim McMannus rose to offer the report. "We picked a theme of the 'Suffering Servant'. And we're hoping to target newly married people, people with young families or young singles searching for meaning in the humdrum of everyday life. We were thinking of perhaps an informal evening type of arrangement with coffee and cookies and maybe questions and discussion after the talks, rather than a longer homily at the Wednesday evening Mass."

Many participants at the three tables indicated agreement with the novel idea. Greg himself concurred, while being preoccupied with her facial expression, sitting at

Intersections

Tim's table. With her chin resting on her propped arms, Eleanor stared at Greg, lost somewhere in past memories, paying little attention to the topic at hand.

"So far, Rob and Marcia have contacted Fr. John Bertaline, the scripture scholar from Catholic University. He's agreed for the third week, and we have calls in to...."

Greg studied her body language as she sat on the end of the second table. He leaned forward over the pedestal half listening to Tim, at the same time trying to watch her without being conspicuous.

The youth committee, the financial committee and the other teams all presented the notes from their individual meetings. Resolutions were offered, voted upon and entered as either passed or tabled for the minutes of this meeting.

"I know I am asking a lot of all of you to come back Thursday night, but Fr. Tim and I will be having visitation with our superior next Tuesday and cannot have the regular meeting." The group agreed to return back two days later.

"So we need to have the list completed and approved so the advertising committee can work on the brochures. Lent is very early this year. Ash Wednesday is February 8." He twirled his finger in the air. "That's just a little over a month from today, so we need things printed and in the pews of the church and in the mail within a couple of weeks."

The enthusiasm in the room energized Greg as he gathered his annotations from the dais. Together he and Tim had built a great team in a short time. Everyone from the committees to the kitchen volunteers to the grounds keepers and greeters were a blessing to work with at the Alverno Retreat House. The two clerics believed and taught that it was the people who made the place, not them. The coming retreats and talks would be successful only because they had good people to help. They could not say it enough in public and individually.

"Thanks for cooking for the kids' fun night, Helen," Greg

moved among the crowd during the time of coffee and cake at the end of the night. Tim circulated also. "And, thanks, John for getting the kids to carry those chairs upstairs the other night." People sensed how much the two priests appreciated each and every person. It was genuine.

Turning while stirring his decaf, Greg bumped her standing very close behind him. His hot drink spilled between them and both jumped apart. "Ouuuu, Eleanor, I didn't see you there." He reached to see if any spilled on her. Eleanor backed away as though terrified that he would touch her. It was contradictory. *She* was the one standing so closely behind him.

Greg brushed off a few drops that made it on his habit and the white cord around him with the three knots. Eleanor made no eye contact, yet during the meeting she could not take her eyes off him. "Hey, thanks for coming up for a few hours this Thursday for Karen."

"What time do you need me, Father?" She still had not fully looked at him, fussing with her own drink, choosing to look past him like a shy teenager.

"Maybe around 2:30. We can get these lists run off for the evening. And if you'd like I'll get us some pizza to eat."

"I'll be there."

"Thanks." Greg reached to touch her arm. This time, she accepted the physical contact, but with trepidation in her gaze.

Wednesday was super busy. Greg celebrated two funerals within five hours at St. Felix for the pastor who was called home with his own family emergency. Final preparations for the visitation the following week were completed. Karen retyped a good copy of his talk for the ecumenical gathering that evening. He looked forward to relaxing with Ray and the friars on Friday. The New Year had started with a bang and already he felt the need for a break.

Intersections

"Hey, Corny, I'll be down for lunch, if that's okay."

"Come on down earlier and concelebrate the 10:00 with all of us. Plus, as I mentioned, you may want to spend some time with Fr. Bede. He's not doing too well."

"Really? That bad?"

"He's come down with a severe case of the flu and has been in bed for days." Ray hesitated, "With his heart and all his other physical complications the doctor says he may not pull out of this one, Greg. He's been pretty well out of it."

"In that case I think I will come early."

"The friars and the seminarians have been keeping a 24-hour prayer watch. You could help with an hour, if you'd like."

"Absolutely, Ray. I definitely will."

"Will you stay the night? You know, they're calling for a good snow later in the day. Nor'easter kind of thing ... sweeping up from the south."

"Probably not. Too much goin' on. And we have visitation with Giles next week."

"You might get stuck down here if it's snows as much as they're saying."

"Nah, I'll ask Tim for his Chevy truck. He's got four-wheel drive. Besides, I have to help again at the parish Saturday as Mark is still gone."

Greg switched the phone to the opposite ear. "Hey, not to change the subject, but I'm pretty certain it's her."

"Why do you say that?"

"Oh, a number of things. And I'm ready to bring it up with her." Greg lowered his voice and twisted the chair towards the back wall of the office. "I'm going to need help for her. And neither Tim nor I would be good. Can you help or suggest someone?"

"I don't know if I'm able ... to get up there regularly and all. But I do have a good contact near you, a psychologist who's good with this kind of emotional problem. And do you think she'll be open to it?"

"Don't know." Greg leaned far back in the swivel chair and bounced it off the edge of the desk. "But I do know this, I *have* to take the chance and say something. For her sake, more than mine. Doesn't bother me anymore." His voice had a lilt. "When the letters stop, I think I'll miss all the sexual flattery."

"You bet, you good looking tiger, you."

"Oh, stuff it, Corney." He swung around in the chair and leaning on the desk switched ears again. "But I've got to tell you that the very last letter, just this week, had something quite interesting that I haven't seen in any of the others."

"What's that?"

"The word, *'again'* like we've been together before or something."

"Huh?"

"Yeah, I'm telling you that almost at the end of every sentence is the word, *'again'*. Like for instance," he picked up the recent letter and read aloud into the phone, "wishing you were lying in bed beside me *again*. And in the following sentence, 'I just want to stroke –"

Karen rapped on the door. Greg stopped in mid-sentence, blushing. He cradled the phone with his chin. "Yes, Karen?"

"I'm goin now, Father. See you Monday morning."

"Hey, have a great time and enjoy Pat ... what's her name."

"Thanks."

"So, Corney she's helping in the office tomorrow, and I'm going to play it by ear. I think it's time. For her sake."

"I'll back you up in prayer."

"See you Friday."

Greg felt uneasy. His sanguine personality rebelled against ambushing anyone. But there was no other way.

The large sheet of paper with the letters *'Y.S.L.'* in bright red from the felt pen was deliberately positioned on the desk in plain view. The stack of letters, the last one unfolded lay close by. Greg vacillated, gathering them back up and placing them in the top drawer. *What if she flies out of here uncontrolled and wrecks or something? Should I wait till after tonight's meeting because she will probably not stay if I ask her before that? What if it wasn't her after all?* The priest's mind raced. Yet, who could challenge her better than he? *I'm the subject of the unrealistic affection and sexual innuendoes.* In all his priesthood he had never encountered such a situation. It was intimidating and enlivening at the same time.

Greg paced back and forth in front of the desk trying to decide. If it were to come to a head, he was the only one to force it. On the other hand, Eleanor would be devastated with sheer humiliation. *Lord, it's your call.* The cleric heard her enter the outer office. He arranged the desk again and went to greet her.

"Can you make about 25 copies of the Lenten Guest Series list for tonight, Eleanor?"

"No problem."

Greg feigned going to the car for something important. "I'll be right back. Just put the copies on my desk"

Eleanor sat in the chair, head down, crying intensely. In her hand was the opened letter.

"Can we talk about this?" Greg sat in the other chair before the desk, gesturing towards what she was holding. Eleanor would not raise her head nor look in his direction. "I would like to help in any way."

Completely devastated by the discovery, Eleanor sobbed, and then meekly laid the letter back on the desk. Still she would not make eye contact with the priest. "I'm so sorry. I didn't mean to hurt or disgrace anybody," she finally faced him, "especially you."

Greg was at a loss for words. His mouth was dry and he really didn't know how to answer now that the situation was in the open. He chose to remain silent and wait.

"I promise you, Father, I didn't want to hurt you. I'm so … so mortified … so humiliated."

"That's okay, Eleanor. I'm just trying to understand … and help in any way possible." Pausing, "I know you have had a rough time since you lost your husband."

"You don't know the whole of it." Eleanor rose, sniffing profusely and went to get her purse from Karen's office. Greg wasn't sure what to do and remained seated. She returned, her hands full of Kleenex, and stood in the middle of the room, frozen in her sorrow, blowing her nose. Being exposed was a relief. "Sometimes I just feel so lost and depressed without him." She dabbed her eyes. "You know it was his anniversary yesterday."

"January 4th?"

"Yeah, three years ago." She spoke through her tears, "and I still miss him so badly sometimes… the kids have moved on … *but I just can't*. He was far too young to go … we had such a good life together." Shaking her head in confusion, "Why, Father, why does God take good people so early?"

Greg delayed and then spoke softly. "And that's why you have transferred all those feelings and so forth to me?"

"To you?" Eleanor responded, looking very mystified "Not really."

The answer confounded Greg. "But, Eleanor, all the letters are sent to me," waving at the display laying on the desk, "with some rather intimate talk I might add."

Now she was very embarrassed. "I know and I do apologize." She would not look at him. "But when you love someone so absolutely and totally as I loved Dave… and were so completely one in body, soul and heart, well …" She was talking to the air with her memories.

Greg was confused. "So, you're not really secretly in love with me?"

"Oh my God, no, Father!" Eleanor turned to him, her hands clutching the crumpled Kleenex up to her mouth. "I

Intersections

never meant to convey that." She lowered her head. "They were *sent* to you, that's true, but they weren't really *addressed* to you."

Greg never noticed from the beginning that there was no salutation. The letters just started without any - 'Dear so-and-so'.

"It was the only way to sooth the grief I still feel so intensely ... reliving memories ... of the letters and intimacy we had as a young couple and throughout our married life." Eleanor sobbed. "And I put it on paper ... and I should have never sent them, but ..."

Greg felt relieved that he wasn't the object of her fantasy. Maybe he *could* be the one to help. But at the same time, that little human bit in any man who thinks he is the Adonis of someone's fantasy was deflated. "But why me, then?"

"Cause you're so good and I knew you wouldn't make it public and ..."

"And?"

"And because ..." She went to her purse again. Standing unassumingly beside him, she handed the picture down to him.

Greg eyes widened. It made sense now. He was out of town at a conference when her husband died and never really met or saw him. Both men looked very much alike, tall, dark black hair, well built. They could have been brothers if not twins.

"How'd he die?"

"A fast-moving brain aneurysm. He was diagnosed right after Christmas that year and died within two weeks. I never had time to say goodbye... and I know three years later ... I should be ... but I get so lonely ... especially some nights ... especially at this time ... writing that stuff helped to relive memories ... oh, I'm so sorry." Sitting, Eleanor placed her face in her hands.

"*We* can talk now that it is in the open. Or I can get

someone for you. There are people who deal specifically with bereavement issues."

She lifted her head. "I think I need that. These past three years have been pure, unmitigated hell."

Greg sought to lighten things. "But I must admit, Eleanor. I was a little flattered thinking it was me."

She flushed and smiled. "Sorry, Father. You are good looking, but it was never you. It's just that... well you reminded me so much of my Dave ... and not just looks ... he was so kind and gentle like you ... so helpful and always cheerful like you and ..."

"Thank you," whispered Greg.

"Actually, Father, you reminded me so much of my Dave that that is why I quit very soon after that and asked you to hire Karen. I couldn't bear to look at you every day and not see him." For the first time she reached and touched his arm. "And Father..."

"What, Eleanor?"

"Please, don't tell Karen."

"Oh, no, of course not. This is between us and whoever I will get to help you sort this out." He decided to hug her. She accepted it. "And don't ever be embarrassed about loving someone so deeply and missing him, but--"

"But what, Father?"

"Can I ask you something?"

"Sure, with what I wrote in those letters, there's not much more to be uncomfortable about."

"What does *Y.S.L.*, that you always signed with, mean?"

Eleanor stepped back from his embrace and locked her hands with the ball of wet tissues. "It was the unique way Dave signed all his notes to me throughout our marriage ... when he gave me a birthday card, a Christmas present, an unexpected bouquet of flowers coming home from work on a Friday afternoon." She faced him. "It means *'Your Secret Lover'*"

They stood silently.

Intersections

"Come on," Greg patted her hand, "it's almost time for tonight's meeting. You okay?"

Eleanor nodded.

Sixteen

It was perfect skiing conditions according to anyone on any level of expertise, a fresh coat of powder overnight, a bright sunny, perfect blue-sky day, crisp sustaining temperatures, little wind. Nancy Collier and Marion Kaieri, a friend from their group at the club, swayed with the chair lift as they followed their respective sons up the intermediate Bobtail Run. Her husband and Bob Rickets were more proficient, choosing to take the expert White Mountain slope over by Apogee Hill.

"Where's Alicia and her friend? I haven't seen much of them today."

"Oh, they're probably still on the beginners' slope. Hunter's never skied and had to take the preliminary lesson. I don't think we'll see them up here today."

"He seems like a nice fellow, Nancy."

Her expression was uneasy, and not too endorsing in her response. "I suppose," she frowned, "don't know a lot about him yet but I guess I will."

Marion caught her hesitation as the two slid with a small

jump from the chair and took their place in line behind the boys to ski down the hill. "He's a senior, isn't he? I think you told me he's graduating this year. Right?"

"Yeah."

"What's he majoring in?"

"I think Alicia said engineering of some kind."

The boys started their own run.

Marion discerned that Nancy wasn't enjoying herself as usual. "You okay?"

"Just a little tired. Alicia and I were up late last night, after everyone went to bed, talking."

"That's nice. She likes him a lot, huh?"

"Yeah."

It was their turn to ski.

Bobtail was a fun ride, some straight downhill but not too much to cause a lot of speed. As an intermediate skier's slope it leveled off with some horizontal bends to help the skier catch their breath and balance before the next down path. The two women stayed close together as they rounded the second bend. Suddenly Nancy, who had done this run tens of times in her life, miscalculated the angle of the curve and fell backwards into the snow.

Marion snowplowed to her side, laughing. "Hey, what happened? You forget those trees were on this bend?"

Nancy lay there, reaching down to re-attach her bootstrap that had broken away causing the left ski to go the length of the cable.

"I'm fine. I was just going too fast for the turn." She struggled with the ski snap and stood up in front of Marion. "She's pregnant."

The bolt from the blue caught her friend off guard. It definitely did not fit the recreation scene, but did explain Nancy's preoccupation. The boys were long gone down the slope. The pleasure of the day was tempered all of a sudden. It made sense to pursue the conversation standing half way down the hill in the snow as skiers of all ages whizzed past them.

"Oh! You sure?"

"I found the torn up box of the pregnancy test in the bathroom waste basket. She tried to rip it into lots of little pieces but I put enough together to read the name. I confronted her last night and she confirmed it…. after some serious prying."

"Is this kid the father?"

Nancy looked annoyed. "I imagine. My daughter's not a promiscuous sleep-a-around like so many others today. I suppose that's why she invited him up here. Maybe they were going to tell us together during his visit."

"Does Harold know?"

"No, and I'm terrified at how he's goin' to react when he *does* find out. I cautioned Alicia not to say any more until it's time to return to school. She and I need time to sort this thing out."

"How long is he staying?"

"Staying till next Wednesday as far as I know. That's what Alicia originally set up, but now I don't know. If this thing tumbles out through some slip of the tongue." Nancy steadied herself and straightened her crooked ski cap. "I just hope I don't give anything away to Harold before me and the kids can come up with a plan." She repeated herself. "I know he's goin' to be furious. Funny, he deals all day long with high school students, kids younger than these guys, who get themselves into all kinds of trouble, and handles them with care and understanding." She faced her. "But I know him too well. It'll be quite different this time, with his *own* daughter!"

Marion Kaieri hugged her friend.

The gigantic, circular fireplace roared from the huge crackling logs trying to be louder than the large group of undergraduates on an outing laughing and shouting across to each other on the surrounding benches. The lobby at

Intersections

Squalors Peak resort was jammed; skiers warming themselves before returning to the slopes, people checking in for the weekend, hotel personnel giving tours of the banquet hall for up coming June weddings. No one in the crowd noticed the two young people way off to the corner of the room sitting silently, heads down in deep thought and firmly holding hands.

"I'll get a job and we'll get married and—"

"Oh, Hunter, be realistic!" Alicia lifted her head. "You only have a semester to go to graduation. You can't quit now."

He squeezed her hands a little tighter, touching the friendship ring he had given her. "Well, I'll just get a part time job and finish the year and then we'll get a place together up there until you finish."

Alicia was upset with his machinations. The entire week Hunter and she have had this same conversation about a hundred times. They tried not letting the family know anything was up, coming up to the resort even though neither of them was in the mood, putting up a lively front in front of everyone.

"My Mom knows."

"Ouuuu." Hunter had immediate mixed feelings.

"She found the pregnancy test package and asked me out right last night."

"And?"

"What do *you* think?" Her eyes expressed frustration. "She's super upset, but—"

"Is she furious at me?"

"No, I don't think so. I mean I don't know. Oh, I don't know anything right now. I'm so confused except that I *do* know—"

"We can get married quietly and no one—"

"No, Hunter, that's what I mean. I *do* know that we *can't* get married right now."

"Why? Don't you love me?" Hunter moved very close to

her face and made direct eye contact.

"Of course I do, but—"

"But what?"

"But getting married right now would only complicate matters with you graduating and all," Alicia smirked and tossed her head, "as though things weren't complicated enough" She lowered her head almost to her lap. "How did I ever let this happen?"

Hunter placed his hand under her chin and gently lifted her head back to eye level. "Hey, hey, stop beating yourself up. We are *both* responsible." He sought to lighten things. "Remember how this thing works. It takes both of us." He looked away past her. "Al- though I thought we were always very cautious about things." Hunter smiled and started to count on his fingers, "except that time after Chad's party, ...and that night in early December after the basketball game and we went to the Ratz Keller to celebrate and ..." Alicia did not smile. "Anyhow, what I mean is that I am with you in this and I will take care of you ... and my responsibilities."

She placed her finger on his lips to quiet him. Vacillating between confusion and calmness, this was a moment of calm. "I know, I know you will, Hunter, but right now we need help and my parents *will* help me ...after they get over the shock and stop being mad and upset."

The noise in the lobby had reached a fierce pitch. A group of college students there for a three-day stay started cheering at the weather report being broadcast on the big TV. The reporter was forecasting the possibility of a large storm coming up the coast, out of the Carolinas, and dumping a ton of snow in the region. Tomorrow's skiing and snow mobile riding would be fantastic.

Normal or low conversation was difficult. Hunter and Alicia sat holding hands, embracing and comforting each other. Noticing the furrowed looks on their faces, people simply smiled at them as though they were young lovers making up from a spat rather than young parents trying to cope with how their lives would soon change. They remained there for over two and a half hours. The throng in the lobby grew, then lessened, and then grew again. It didn't matter at all to Hunter and Alicia. They sat rehearsing in their minds the answers they would give if and when the news became public, and sustaining each other in silence.

As the noise in the large area softened again in direct contrast to the fire bursting into a new surge with fresh logs added by the manager, Alicia finally broke the quiet. "There's something else you should know, Hunter."

"What?"

There was a long pause.

"Well..." Alicia appeared to have a number of things to say. She hugged him to help brace him against what she was about to disclose. "Well ...I know you're goin' to be mad at me but I have to tell you."

"Yeah?"

"I'm ... I'm ...not goin' back to school."

Hunter pushed her away arms length. "What!"

"I can't be at school and pregnant at the same time. I haven't told my folks that either but I think I'll be here until the baby is born and..."

"And?"

"And figure out something. I don't know. I'm just so confused."

Hunter was destroyed. Not only was she not on board with his wanting to get married immediately, Alicia was not going to be with him for the final semester. In all the conversations about the situation, this was the worst. "But I wouldn't be able to live without you, see you every day, hold you."

Alicia schussed him again with one finger on his lips. "Hunter, you know I couldn't study and be pregnant. Don't worry I'll finish ... someday. Right now I'm just too overwhelmed to even think about school."

Hunter tried a compromise with rambling thoughts. "I'll graduate and come back here then and we'll get married here and get our own place and I'll take care of the baby and work at night so you can finish school and ..."

A third time his lips were sealed with her soft finger. They just held each other.

The ride back home to Newark was quiet except for Brian and his Dad both boasting about how they conquered new slopes on this day and how much more they intended to do in the future until the highest mountain was mastered. Nancy, her daughter and Hunter said very little. Nancy rode in the passenger seat beside her husband, stealing furtive glances and speculating how his mood would change immensely with the news. Hunter sat behind Harold caressing his daughter, leaning on his chest as Brian bounced by the opposite window. Hunter tried to study her Mom. Nancy would not look at him when she spoke as little as she did about the day. Brian asked for a certain type of music for the radio. His Dad conceded. It filled the void, however inconsistent it was, with what plagued their hearts.

Rubbing his hurting angles from the little bit of skiing that he did do that morning, and applying Ben Gay, Hunter sat on Brian's bed in his boxer shorts. It was nearly midnight and as tired as he was, he could not sleep worrying about Alicia, and especially being upset that she was not returning this semester. Before he knew it the digital clock, also with some sort of NCAA logo, flipped to 1 AM. He lay back on the pillow on top on the covers when someone knocked lightly. It was Alicia. She also could not sleep.

"Hi," he whispered.

"Hold me."

"Okay." He closed the door and they stood embracing. Both of them clasped the half heart pendants around their necks in solidarity. Together they held them together to make a complete one. "You feel okay? No upset stomach or anything."

"No, I feel fine physically. Just totally mixed up inside." She put her head on his chest. The strong rhythm of his heart soothed her in preparation for her next statement. "My Mom and Dad's door's been closed all night. I think she's telling him even though she promised to wait a little bit until we could talk together."

"Or maybe they're gettin' it on."

The effort to cause her to laugh amidst this heavy state of affairs worked. Alicia snickered and hit him with her fist. "Hunter!"

"Well, if your Mom's telling him, I'm right here to accept my responsibility in person... unlike *my Dad!*"

Alicia and he had thrashed out the story between his parents for hours, both at school and here amidst the other worries. She had not met his folks yet but tried to envision what they were like. Hunter was completely let down by his Dad and she was the only one with whom he could fully share his hurt. He slipped in the sarcasm many times in their conversations. "Shhhh, shhhh, shhhh, Hunter, be cool. You just may not know the whole story."

"Dammit. I know the whole story, okay. My Mom's having his baby and he's abandoning her." It was the first time Hunter realized that both his Mom and his girlfriend were pregnant at the same time.

Alicia and he sat on the bed, propped up against the headboard with their feet stretched out and entwined in each other's arms. The moments became an hour and before they knew it, both drifted off to sleep from exhaustion.

It was 5 a.m. when the second knock of the night came. It was not as gentle as the first. The noise startled Alicia and Hunter as they realized they had fallen asleep. Afraid to be discovered in Brian's room on the bed together, Alicia froze as Hunter jumped up. He motioned for her to get in the closet. She bolted to it, closing the door behind her. Hunter, still in his boxers, cautiously opened shielding most of his body behind the door in case it was her Mom.

"Young man, get dressed!" Harold stood there completely dressed himself with a furious scowl on his face, fists clenched down in front of him.

"What?"

"Get you stuff together, right now. I want you out of here as soon as possible. You and I are leaving for the bus station in 40 minutes. I've called and there's a bus to Harrisburg at 6:30 and you *will* be on it!" The tone of his voice was harsh. "From there you can switch to a bus for Ohio."

"But sir ..."

"Don't you *sir* me. You didn't respect my daughter. So I do not respect you!" He turned and walked briskly away from the door. "40 minutes ... out in the driveway!"

Alicia came out of the closet, crying. They clung to each other. "Oh, my God, I am so sorry, Hunter. He's blaming you for everything!"

"Shhhh, shhhh," it was his turn to cover her lips with an index finger. "It's goin' to be all right. He's just a little shocked right now and--."

"A little!"

"Well ... a lot but I'll go now like he says and when things settle down, I'll come back and we will hack this out with them together. I promise."

Alicia felt his strength and squeezed harder, not wanting to ever let go of him. "I love you."

Mr. Collier held the car door for Hunter to place his duffle on the back seat. He closed it forcefully and headed around the car to the driver's side.

Despondently, Alicia stood at her bedroom window twisting the friendship ring back and forth on her finger.

"Sir, I love your daughter very much and I accept my..."

Her Dad turned the corner from their street. "You don't

know what love is, young man. You think love is all sweet talk, and good feelings and getting my daughter into bed and..."

Hunter respectfully interrupted. "Sir, it did not happen that way. We *really* do love each other and I accept my responsibility and am willing to marry your—"

"Marry! No way! You're not even graduated. You don't have a degree, or a job, or a place to live. Marry! You guys are so far from that, it isn't funny."

"But there's lots of couples that started from nothing and turned out to have a long life together."

"Not my daughter! No way, son. We'll take care of this, thank you. And I would trust that you would just stay away, not call or anything. You have ruined my daughter's life right now."

Hunter objected again in a respectful way. "But, sir, that is my child and I *will* take responsibility... unlike my Dad!"

Mr. Collier did not understand the meaning of the last words. He was too blinded with fury at the moment to even ask.

"First this," he snapped, "and then I find out that you are *not* majoring in engineering, but rather liberal arts. What I want to know is what else have you deceived Alicia's mother and me about?"

Hunter remained silent, his mouth open, his eyes squinted.

There would be no more conversation on the way to the bus station. Mr. Collier reached and turned on the radio, loud. The news spoke again of the impending snowstorm.

Hunter was sick inside. No way did he want to go home this down and discouraged. But it was best right now to shut up and let Alicia's folks have some time to settle down.

The terminal was winter dark and desolate except for a few early travelers, not the bustle like when he arrived. It took time to re-do his ticket to accommodate his leaving earlier than planned. If the snow held off not causing the

Jim Caldwell

trip to be delayed or slowed, they should be in Harrisburg early afternoon. He could find a bus to Mentor from there.

Crestfallen, Hunter took the very last seat on the left in the half empty bus. Laying his head against the window as they pulled from the terminal, he watched the early morning lights in Newark going on in building after building as they dwindled in sight. Reaching under his t-shirt, he pulled out the gold chain with the pendant and cross, gripping it in a fist against his heart. The distance grew between him and Alicia and their unborn baby with every minute. Hunter slouched down in a coiled position as though he just wanted to hide and make all the hurt disappear. He hid his pain even from the empty seats.

Seventeen

Greg pulled the long white alb over his head and hung it on the hook in the cabinet. A confrere laid a hand on his shoulder.

"Hey, good to see ya, Greg. How ya been?" Colin Morriston, one of the concelebrants at the liturgy, asked.

"Good, Morry, how you doin' teaching these guys at the seminary?"

"Great, I love it. You busy up at the retreat house?"

"Super busy, but I have a fantastic team."

Colin patted his shoulder twice as he waved and left the sacristy. Others greeted Greg, welcoming him. Ray finished taking his vestments off and turned to him. "Ready for some lunch?"

"You know I was thinking of spending time with Fr. Bede right away. I'm not really that hungry, and besides," he motioned out the chapel window, "that snow's looking a little more ominous, so I may not stay as long as I planned."

"Why don't you stay the night?"

Jim Caldwell

"Told you, Corney, I can't. Got far too much to do. Almost cancelled coming down today except that I wanted to see Bede and pray for him."

"Okay. No problem."

Greg rubbed his hands as though they were cold. "By the way, Ray, great homily. I loved your idea that the Epiphany of the Lord is only the beginning of showing himself to us throughout our lives," he said tilting his head and raising the right eyebrow, "and that we should joyfully expect constant, surprise revelations. Thanks for the reminder!"

"Learned from the best. Some old experienced retreat master I've known for a few years."

"Old ... getting there. Experienced ...maybe ... that's up for discussion." The priests laughed with each other.

Greg pushed the partially opened door slowly. It was dark in the tiny room. Franciscan writings often referred to the Friars' quarters as 'cells'. That term was meant to describe the simplicity of their bedroom, not with any connotation of a prison. Fr. Bede's cell was as plain as it could be, space only for a bed, a desk with a small green lamp, no furnishings on the walls except a San Damien crucifix, dark maple wood shutters on the single window, and a bare wooden floor, a room the priest had slept and prayed in for the last twenty-three years of his life. The lower half shutter was fastened shut letting only a sliver of light pierce the room from the opened top portion.

Only one hard-backed book from the monastery library, the *Life of St. Joseph Leonissa,* lay on the desk, reminiscent of the novitiate days when a friar was taught to concentrate fully on a single spiritual tome at a time. A college seminarian sat beside the bed, eyes closed in meditation. He roused with Greg's entrance.

"Oh, hi, Father."

"If it's okay with you, I'll take my turn and you can get some lunch, if you'd like."

"Sure." The young student closed the prayer book on his lap, slipped back into his loafers and left the room as quietly as Greg had entered.

Fr. Bede lay there, in a suspended state, eyes shut firmly, his mouth dry and cracked opened, arms down at his side under the course brown blanket. His frail, small-sized body barely reached the bottom of the bed. The large, black-beaded rosary, usually hanging on the side of his habit, instead straddled the bedpost. There was very little motion, hardly any sound except an occasional guttural rasp as he heaved for breath. The priest's countenance was neutral and bland, the face of an elderly person asleep, registering neither pain nor giving little hint that this saintly man was near death.

Greg took the hard chair beside the bed, opened his collar for comfort, placed his folded hands over his mouth and studied the figure before him. He smiled kindly at the sight of Fr. Bede's proverbial gray, straggly goatee barely visible above the cover. *Hello, Fr. Bede. I've come to pray with you.* It was the customary salutation for years as he visited the old man for spiritual direction. Greg was half expecting his mentor lying there so motionless to come back with his usual reply: *How's your spiritual life these days?* He did not shift even an eyebrow.

Snowflakes the size of heavy raindrops fell past the upper windowpane. Greg knew he better head back up route 83 within the next couple of hours or risk being stuck there overnight. The snow seem to fall in strong bands of blinding white, then settle back to a very light pattern.

"They should be able to stay ahead of the roads," Greg mumbled out loud as though Fr. Bede were listening. He chose to pray the noon time hour of the breviary first before meditating. The time passed with nary a peep except the squeak of the desk chair when Greg shifted his weight.

Praise your name, Lord, for the life of this man, he implored as he closed the clerical book. *And I thank you for all the times you revealed yourself to me through this holy man, the times you forgave my sins through him, the times you comforted me from my nightmares.* Greg was peaceful in his solitude, yet doubted who could ever take Fr. Bede's place as his spiritual director.

"Gregory."

Greg reacted with stark bewilderment. It was the first sign of any verve from the man in the bed. Yet, Fr. Bede's eyes remained closed tight; there was no movement whatsoever in his body. He rose quickly and bowed down over the sickly man. "Yes, Father?"

There was no answer. Did he imagine that Fr. Bede had called his name? "I've come to pray with you," he said. In spite of everything there was no change. Greg sat back down and heaved a deep sigh. The sensation in his stomach was the same he had seven years ago when he was called home to Philly by his younger sister and spent two days and nights beside his Dad's bed.

He deserves your light, Lord, for a job well done, Greg entreated now with his own eyes closed in reflection. The hour slipped by swiftly. *Take him home to be with you always, Father.*

"Gregory."

The old man spoke again. Greg popped up a second time.

His name was said in a very low, throaty voice. Greg barely heard it in the entirely quiet room. "She is okay, Gregory. The Father holds her in his arms." Still no open eyes; even now no movement of any other part of his body.

Silence again.

Greg knew the words referred to the Vietnam trauma and his life long nightmare. Laying his hand on the cover over the old priest's hand underneath, he prayed. "Thank-you." The man, whom Greg relied on for solace in those painful moments of depression, would play the role till to the last sentence uttered.

Someone rapped lightly and entered. "I will stay now, Father, if you need to go." Another friar had signed on for the one o'clock hour. "How is he?"

"Peaceful."

Greg made the sign of the cross on Fr. Bede's forehead as he imparted his personal blessing and headed for the door. The new vigil keeper sat on the wooden chair.

"He is okay too, Gregory."

Once again the tone with the harsh German accent was so low and garbled that neither visitor in the room was certain what was muttered. Greg returned to the foot of the bed, both friars staring at the face on the flat pillow. Nothing was repeated.

Does he mean Duane? Greg speculated.

Fr. Bede appeared to open his eyes slightly and smile at them. The light was so dim in the room that neither could be sure they saw what they thought they saw.

"Who, Fr. Bede?"

Rotating his head slowly to the left, he slept. The two friars waited patiently for more activity or speech, then Greg decided to leave, aware that it would be the final time he would see his spiritual director.

People were driving unbearably slow on the interstate. Even though it was a four-lane highway, traffic crawled. *Come on, folks, stop riding your breaks. Worst thing to do in snow,* Greg mouthed impatiently, slapping his palms on the top of the steering wheel. His collarbone was sore from the strain that winter driving causes many a driver. Greg massaged it with his right hand and rolled his neck.

Periodically the municipal trucks went down or up, spraying salt and scrapping, but the bands were coming with regularity now and within minutes it was as though the thoroughfare had had no attention at all. Greg drove well in snow and Tim's truck was solid; it was the other drivers he was nervous about, those not composed while driving under precarious conditions.

Camp Hill. This misery shouldn't be much longer.

The flashing reds and blues cut the wintry landscape with grim reality, a sight that would spark fear in anyone. The alarming emergency lights were concentrated up ahead on the turnpike to the right of exit 18, the Harrisburg West shore interchange.

Greg, the seasoned spiritual minister that he was, immediately thought how he could help. Stretching over to the glove compartment of Tim's Chevy, he banged the knob, dropping it open. *Good.* He identified the small black, familiar case with the holy oils. *Good. Tim does have them in here.*

Everyone was moving at a snail's pace. Greg devised his next step when he spotted the two vehicles racing up along side towards him. An ambulance, followed very closely by a Pennsylvania State Police car, sped up the berm with sirens whaling incessantly, provoking a new rush of adrenaline.

Call it instinct. Greg swung the truck out of line causing the cop to turn sharply to avoid colliding with his front fender, hit his flashers and tailed them with the same intensity. Sergeant Baracka scowled at him in the rear view mirror, but barreled towards the destination.

"Who the hell!"

The parade of emergency vehicles zoomed up the down ramp and through the tollgate going the wrong direction. Highway personal made the unorthodox entry possible by blocking the way to all others. Greg followed despite the glares from the turnpike workers, who allowed him through nonetheless.

The accident was on the westbound side, but for the time being the entire freeway in both directions was stopped, permitting only authorized personnel to get to the scene. All three in single file raced up the east lanes, bouncing across the small v-shaped strip towards the crash. The EMS leading the pack veered in place beside the other

Intersections

ambulances. Sergeant Baracka, conscious of the busy area, backed down into the snow-covered median and jumped out. Greg swerved beside him.

"What the hell!" Baracka angrily yelled at Greg, as two other officers approached them.

"I'm a Catholic priest. If I could help in any way?"

"Okay," he saw Greg's collar, "damn, you know I almost caught your front end. Didn't you see me?"

He barked at the policemen who joined them. "Clear the middle lane as soon as possible and get things moving. But keep the far one clear to the ramp for the ambulances to exit. And tell them also to let the eastbound go. Move the rubberneckers along! Or we'll have a larger parking lot than we need!"

The storm settled down, a subtle mixture of wet snow and ice. A trooper stood near the semi involved in the accident, interviewing a very distraught driver who was chain-smoking cigarettes. Three of the five ambulances had their rear doors wide open, emergency technicians attending people for various wounds. The fourth one already at the scene had its doors closed, preparing to transport one or more severely injured riders. The newly arrived EMT's rushed to a few travelers left sitting in open backseats of the patrol cars, several still sitting on the ground in damp snow near the overturned bus.

"Can I pray for you? Are you catholic? Would you like me to bless you?" Greg started with the nearest opened ambulance. A male in his twenties nodded that he was not catholic but said that his Mom was being attended to inside the van and would like a blessing. *"It would calm her down,"* were his exact words.

Greg moved from passenger to passenger, giving priority to the more seriously injured that wanted to be prayed over or comforted. Spiritual solace in a trauma does help to dispel shock. Medical staff permitted Greg free rein. He respected their work and stayed within bounds of "not being in the road."

Most of the ambulances had now transported people to the Harrisburg hospital center and returned. Those less injured were asked to travel in the vans to the emergency room for a thorough check-up. Traffic was again moving on both sides alleviating some congestion, although still only one lane was opened westbound. A burly tow truck driver from a local garage navigated into place to upright the bus, lying on its side with the back half hanging precariously over the hill. The coroner likewise had arrived.

Baracka come up to Greg, climbing out of the last remaining ambulance, the falling precipitation giving his black hair a crust of white around the edges, his face dripping wet. "There are a couple of fatalities, Father. Both were seated towards the back of the bus. Would you like to pray over them?"

"Yes."

Two sheet-covered bodies lay on litters awaiting transport. For a moment he flashed back to Vietnam and the numerous war-torn scenes of death and destruction. It gripped him but he could not let it affect his duties. Greg lifted the sheet from the one nearest him. It was a badly bruised woman, very obese, mid-thirties, and a thin wedding ring on her finger. The priest anointed her forehead with the holy oils and quickly moved to the second stretcher.

He suffered a blunt trauma to the head. Dried blood covered the right temple. His coat and shirt were ripped and heavily stained; his broken fist jammed under his chin. The young man clutched a chain with a cross and a small heart charm. Greg fingered the silver cross, turning it over and reading the traditional phrase often embossed on the religious symbol: *'In case of an accident, please call a priest'. Mmmmm*, he thought, *whoever gave him this, must have loved him dearly.* Greg anointed the body with a little more fervor, rubbing the oil on the five senses of his eyes, ears, nostrils, lips and hands, assured he was catholic and perhaps his loved ones would be grateful for the sacrament, if they asked and were informed. As he came to the battered hand, Greg inadvertently touched the heart pendant as he made the sign of the cross with his thumb. It never occurred to him that he had touched the deceased young man less than a week ago when the two bumped into each other at the bus station. "Through this holy unction may the Lord pardon you whatever sins or faults you may have committed …"

The trooper who had filed the statement with the truck driver moved toward him. "Father."

"Yes."

"Can I have your name and some information for the accident report? The family is oftentimes very consoled when they are told that a member of the clergy stopped at the scene."

"Sure. Fr. Greg Pugh. P_u_g_h." He spelled it. "Alverno Retreat Center. 2348 North Route 15. Millersburg, Penn.…" The officer wrote. "The zip code: 17061."

Baracka walked over to them. The emergency was pretty well cleared except for Coroner Mullaugher directing the bodies to the morgue and the removal of the bus from the highway. Traffic in the westbound lanes was picking up.

"Open all traffic lanes," he ordered nearby police officers. Addressing Greg, "Thanks, Father." The sergeant started for his car. "Oh, and I'm sorry for barking at you the way I did."

"What happened?" Greg asked, stopping Baracka in his tracks as he turned back towards him.

"A brief whiteout, like it's been all day. The driver of the 18-wheeler was traveling a little too fast for conditions. By the time he realized he was over too far in the other lane, he clipped the back of the bus causing it to swerve and topple." Waving his hand high in the air. "It could have been a lot worse. Lots more fatalities. Believe me, we were lucky with only two."

Jim Caldwell

Greg nodded in agreement. The pair reached their respective vehicles in the median. A turnpike worker, cleaning up the debris on the road, blocked the way for their exit out of the middle of the strip.

Ray telephoned around 10:00 that night to say that Fr. Bede had passed into eternal life. Greg typed the notice about the funeral and prayers to be recited by the community in the next days and posted it on the bulletin board outside the recreation room.

The storm never completely ended until after midnight. Weather forecasters gave eight inches as the total official number. At dinner Greg relayed his being at the accident on the news to his brothers.

No one involved in calamities ever walks away with a sense of inner joy, but there still is a sense of accomplishment that in some way you helped someone in their desperate time of need. For a priest, who participates as the bridge between God and man in the most intimates of life's spiritual moments – baptism, marriage, death – there is an especially satisfying sense of purpose. Greg climbed into bed whispering a prayer for the injured, and in particular the victims of the accident and their families.

Weary from the whole day's experiences, he fell asleep not recognizing that on this same day, the feast of the Epiphany of the Lord, he had lost both his spiritual father and his own 21-year-old flesh and blood son.

Eighteen

Lonnie grasped her mother's hand tighter, handing her more Kleenex, her own eyes as red and swollen as the other three women. Lynn, prodded by Elena, who was concerned for the safety of the pregnancy, tried to persuade Julie to stretch her legs out on the sofa. The phone call totally shattered the girls' trying to convince their mother that she was not *too old* to have a baby shower. The twins had been excited about planning one with favors and games and all. They had earlier that very day convinced Darlene's Mom to help them.

"Oh, my God! It can't be. It just can't be! My Hunter isn't coming home till next Wednesday." Julie gave up the soggy clump of tissues for the new batch. "Please tell me it isn't my son." Rambling to each one over and over. "Lonnie, tell me it's not your brother." She reached for Lyn's hand as her daughter stood behind the couch. "They're telling me Hunter's dead. It can't be!" Her sobbing was heart wrenching. "Did you call your Dad again? ... What was that gentleman's name on the phone again? Oh, I'm so confused."

"Shush, Mom, shush. Maybe you're right. Maybe they'll call back and tell us it's just a mistake and they got the wrong name." Lonnie knelt on one knee, clinging to her Mom's arm, leaning her head against Julie's tear streaked cheek. Lynn wanted to run from the room, the house, and the world to satiate the vicious pit in her stomach. Elena non-verbally assured the daughters that it was okay to let Julie ramble.

Shock needs a place to vent.

Lynn paced back and forth before slipping from the room. She had to *do* something, anything. She called Darlene.

"Take me to him, Elena." Now Julie grabbed up at her longtime friend. "I've got to see him. I've got to know." She clutched Lonnie's arm. "We have to call Alicia, honey. What's her last name again?" No one answered. "And the university … Oh, God, I can't bear to call there and all his friends! This is his graduation year. I was going to have a gigantic picnic up on the lake." Julie paused for a long time, staring and looking at nobody. "Oh, and girls, I still have stuff in the dryer downstairs. We have to take it out and hang it up so it's not overly wrinkled." Her thoughts were everywhere and nowhere.

She gestured in the air to Lynn who had already left. "Please try your Dad again."

Deep anguish and sorrow creates incoherency.

Elena was the strong one among them at the moment. It was impractical to head for Harrisburg at 8 o'clock on a winter's night, perhaps heading into the very storm they say caused the accident.

Besides no one official would be at the place until morning. Could she convince the three to wait till the next day?

"Lonnie, did you call your Dad like I asked you?"

"Yes, Mom, twice but I didn't get him. Both times they said he was tied up in court. … I'll try again."

Intersections

"Dammit! On a Friday afternoon! Ridiculous! Where the hell is he?"

The anger phase of grief was weaving in and out of Julie's feelings.

"Where is he when I need him the most?"

"That's what they said, Mom." Lonnie cried the answer.

"Go, call again, he might be back now." Julie missed what her daughter had just said. "Call his apartment. Call the office again. No, they will be gone. Oh, what time is it, anyways?"

"A little after eight, Mom."

She heaved a deep breath. It was as though for a brief moment, she might be in the stage of pity. "Please. Your Dad needs to know as soon as you can get a hold of him." She rubbed her stomach in a soft circular motion as she pushed herself up from the sofa with her other hand. "And Elena, help me go upstairs and check to see how Hunter's blue sports coat looks. I may have to have it cleaned to lay ..." She quickly slumped back down in despair. She felt like she wanted to vomit, but said nothing. Elena deciphered her face and brought a glass of water with an Alka-Seltzer.

Lonnie left to call Russell. Lynn returned, taking her place clutching to her Mom's arm. Elena helped her recline her legs up on the two throw pillows.

"Dear God, help us ... take care of my Hunter ... Elena, please take me to him" Julie pleaded. "I know it's not going to be him. It's someone who looks like him. He's not coming home till next week." Glancing up, "Lynn I think their last name is Collins ... no, it's Collier." Julie pointed to the hallway. "Hunter gave me a phone number. I left it on the desk, honey. Go and call your brother at the Collier's place." Pausing for a silent moment of reflection, Julie whispered "I was so glad you guys didn't call him about me being in the hospital this week. I didn't want to bother him. I know he loves that girl and he's enjoying himself at their home."

Her stomach settled.

"It'll be alright, Mom." Lynn hugged her and hung on.

There is never a convenience store handy when you need one. Elena drove three blocks out of their way at the entrance to the Ohio turnpike for gas and to get another box of tissue, aspirin, a small travel tube of toothpaste and some ginger ale. She worried that Julie might dehydrate from the shock and strain. She was concerned about the stress on the baby.

Standing outside, with a fist full of coins, Elena confirmed the motel room immediately off exit 10 in Pennsylvania. The compromise would be to stay somewhere halfway and go in the morning to identify Hunter. Traveling at night would help assuage the nervous acid churning inside Julie and her twins. Death, and especially sudden death, produces sourness in the gut. Driving part of the way would alleviate some of the angst.

"Here is some change. Try your Dad again. He has to be there by now."

Lonnie dialed. No answer. Both of them groaned with irritation.

"Remember that time, Lynnie, when Timmy Harkins," squeezing her daughter's hand out and in like a ball pump, "and those boys up the street took yours and Lonnie's Halloween candy and your brother went charging up there." Julie cracked a grin, the first time since the phone call, clenching her tissues and talking loud, letting go of Lynn's hand and putting her fist to her chin. "Your brother was going to beat the pulp out of him." The smile broadened a little further. "My peace-loving Hunter was going to stick up for his little sisters."

Julie uncrossed her feet across Lonnie's lap on the back seat. Lynn sat in the passenger seat, reaching her hand back to her Mom.

"Oh, God! Why! He was such a good kid! He didn't do anything wrong. Why, Lord, why!"

The despair phase.

Julie crushed Lynn's hand and pointedly looked to each of her daughters. "Oh, how he loved you guys."

The fetus felt the anger and frustration and shifted inside her womb. Julie flinched. "He loved life so much. Did we get in touch with Alicia yet? I forget. Is she also a senior?"

"Don't know, Mum."

"Hunter was going to ask her to come stay with us during spring break."

Elena saw the first signs of snow on the windshield as they crossed the Pennsylvania line. The last vestiges of the storm were dissipating little by little, sweeping northeast out of the keystone state.

Exit 4, Butler.

Elena gently announced the plan to stay off the highway overnight. No one protested. The exhaustion from grief, pain, tension and disbelief and grief and pain again brought a tiredness that overwhelmed them. Yet, no one would completely sleep, especially Julie.

Three more calls to Russell from the motel room. Three more times the phone rang forever without being answered.

"Damn you, Russell!" Julie rubbed her forehead and wiped her eyes. "All I'm asking is that you be there ... be here. We need you." She coughed and sniffled. "And we have to call Hunter's roommate. And Lynn, did you call Alicia?"

"No, Mom, we'll call them when we get back tomorrow. I don't have those phone numbers with us."

The endless loop of chatter, when someone is nervous and dealing with death, is bewildering and therapeutic at the same time. "Do you girls remember that big wide, red tie with the little silver speckles in it that your Dad and I brought him for his Confirmation?" Julie chuckled. "No, you wouldn't remember. You guys were only nine or ten. It was as bright as his face and we honestly thought he would like it. But your brother hated it. Said it was 'out of style and embarrassed him'. Then he insisted on wearing it for his eighth-grade graduation a couple of months later ... because he thought *we* would like it. " Shaking her head, "Elena, tell me the truth. Do you think we should put a tie on him? He never really liked wearing a tie, you know. Shouldn't we do what he would like this time? Right?"

The questions were rhetorical; the memories were many as sheer fatigue finally quieted the room.

A new day. Sunshine can made a storm a bad dream but does nothing to stomp out the grief left in its wake. Nothing could erase the fact that they were going to a *morgue – the very sound of the word was harsh and ugly* --- where Julie had to identify her firstborn.

They showered. They ate at the pancake house across the street from the motel; even Julie had a little something.

There were more reminiscences. "Elena, I remember the first time Russell and I had Hunter in a motel when he was little." Julie put up her hands towards the girls, waving at them slightly. "You guys weren't even born at the time. Hunter thought it was absolutely fantastic having the TV in the same room as the bed where we would sleep. It never occurred to him that a motel room is only one room with a small bathroom. He wanted to stay there the next morning and just watch cartoons from bed instead of getting back on the road for the beach."

All of them climbed up and down the rungs of bereavement, each in their own time frame.

Lonnie was angry. Julie consoled.

Lynn would not believe it. Elena softly listened.

The mother was resigned and she and her daughters were on the same phase, recalling fond memories.

Julie was bargaining with God. Lonnie and Lynn soothed her.

Death alone puts forward a vast mystery but a sudden death, particularly a person in the prime of his life, is completely unfathomable.

It was time to go. The miles were long; the ride was slow and distressing. Two more exasperating phone calls to Russell at rest stops. No answer.

"Elena, remind me to call Phil from Harrisburg."

"Okay. And who is Phil?"

"Russell and I have known him for years. He will handle the arrangements. We laid my Mom out there and Russell's sister-in-law three years ago when she died of breast cancer." Julie was coming to grips with the decisions that needed to be made. "Oh, and Lonnie, we have to call Fr. Kearns and your school and ..."

"Okay, Mom."

South 28th Street was practically deserted. There is no business done at the courthouse on Saturday. Parking in front of the place was not only allowed on weekends but was also free. Elena was concerned with finding the side door they were told to enter for the morgue downstairs. They were told to ring the bell marked at that entrance. She strained to see if they were on the right side of the building. Lonnie helped Julie from the car. Lynn felt nauseated with frightful butterflies. Only Julie saw him at first. It immediately gave her strength ... the strength she needed for this task.

Russell stood waiting for them at the top of the steps.

There are many wounds in life that words do not heal only actions can do that. With the help of the twins, Julie ascended to him and in a tableau setting, husband and wife, Hunter's parents, simply embraced tenaciously. She concealed her face in Russell's chest, quietly sobbing. He rested his chin on her slightly disheveled hair, weeping, lips tightly held together and teeth clenched to keep control. Reaching out with one hand for his daughters, they formed a wider embrace, inviting Elena into the fold. No words were spoken, only the touch of five individuals adding power to the whole. The only sounds were the humiliating sniffs produced with crying. One minute became six before the circle broke.

"Ready?"

"Yes, Russell, I'm ready."

The anteroom was ominous. One could only imagine what the real lab was like with the cold silver tables and wall drawers. Lynn wanted to throw up. Lonnie thought how naïve it was that she and her date joined the group who went to the morgue after the prom last year when she was a sophomore. *How stupid we were,* she thought.

A professional looking staff person, a man in his upper fifties, very short gray hair and stocky, small, gold-rimmed glasses sitting half way down his nose, and dressed in a long white lab coat that practically dragged on the floor, came out, extending his hand in sympathy. "Mr. and Mrs. Harrisson?"

They rose, Russell supporting his wife.

"I really only need one to identify the body. Would that be you, Mr. Harrisson?"

He shook his head. But Julie protested. "I want to go with you."

Russell agreed and the two followed the man into the long, brightly lit room with what seemed like a million florescent lights and down along the mausoleum looking wall. Glancing first at the note in his hand for the proper place, the gentleman walked almost to the end as they nervously followed. He checked the number once more. Then gripping the handle tightly with both hands, the man pulled the drawer open. Julie gasped and collapsed quickly into Russell's arms. He nodded in the affirmative with a few jerks of his head up and down, biting his lower lip. The attendant closed it.

"Can I ask you please to return to the anteroom? I'll need a few moments to finish the paper work and have you sign, --- sorry we are always shorthanded on the weekends --- and then I'll retrieve his personal affects for you to take. Do you folks have a particular funeral director to come for the body... and perhaps a phone number or address? And will he be coming from Ohio?"

Julie looked up at her husband. "McPhearson's." Russell concurred.

He helped her out the double doors. The worst was over.

"Here are the clothes he was wearing, and his belongings."

Lynn broke out crying with the sight of the Garrison duffle bag. Having not been inside, this was the reality punch for her and her sister. Elena hugged them.

"And Mrs. Harrisson."

Julie was rising from the hard bench with help from Russell.

"Here are the individual items he had on his person." The gentleman handed her the clear plastic bag.

Julie sat back down and looked carefully at it. She held the half heart pendant. "Ah, we have to call Alicia tonight. She is going to so broken up. I feel sure she loved him." She spoke to no one in particular. Russell continued to support her with his arm around her.

After reading the words on the back and sighing, Julie brought the cross close to her lips and closed her eyes.

"Ma' m."

"Yes."

"There *was* a catholic priest that stopped at the accident and helped. The report said he anointed your son."

Julie clutched the cross, kissing it. "God bless you, Aunt Isabel," she whispered to no one but herself. "Do you have his name?"

"No, Ma'm, I do not have the police report down here in this office, but I could have someone upstairs send you a copy on Monday."

"I would like that."

She turned to Russell. "We better go."

It was Julie's request. When they reached the turnpike, Russell headed east to the very next exit, then swung back on the highway going west. They approximated the spot, pulled over with blinkers and spent a poignant moment of silence where they construed that Hunter was killed.

Resignation is yet another step in the grieving process.

The last one, acceptance, would be the hardest.

The evening was tough with painful phone calls, especially the one to Alicia and her family. Fr. Kearns had set a 10:00 Tuesday Mass and relatives and friends were notified one by one.

Russell and Julie talked late into the night after Elena and the girls had gone to bed, reconciling, sharing memories of their son and crying together.

She reached for his hand. "Thank-you."

"God, I have been such an idiot. Can you ever forgive me?"

"Shsssss, you're here. That's what counts right now. I need you. I realized yesterday how much I need you in my life."

"And I need you." He squeezed her to him, and they just held each other in silence.

"But how did you find out what happened?" She stayed in his arms.

"Danielle said Lynn sounded very upset when I got back to the office. My first thought was that there was something up with you and the baby. I hurried past the house. But you and Elena and the girls had already left. I was confused as to what was going on when I saw Darlene running down the street. She told me that Lynn had called her and told her what had happened and you had to go to Harrisburg to identify Hunter."

Russell placed his lower lips over top the upper one for a moment. "I took a commuter plane this morning at 5 a.m. and..."

He hesitated and hugged her tighter. "I miss him so much already and I am *so* sorry I ever left... I love you..."

Nineteen

The story of the tragedy made the front page of the local newspaper in Mentor. As a result many strangers called or sent cards offering sympathy, and the affection displayed for Hunter by folks in the small town was overwhelming. Both nights at McPhearson's were jam-packed with family from all parts of the country, people from both places of work, classmates from the girls' high school, neighbors, and car loads of friends from Garrison as well as a couple of professors who drove down with them. Even 94-year-old Mr. Baughman asked his son from Cleveland to drive him to pay his respects to "that happy-go-lucky kid who would cut his grass and accept nothing in return except to share half a baloney sandwich with him and tell him funny stories."

Fr. Kearns remarked at the liturgy that the number of young people present was an excellent testimonial to Hunter's giving personality. He reminded them to always celebrate life in positive ways since no one "knows neither the day nor the hour." Brian Parks had the crowded church smiling and chuckling with personal thoughts of his best friend and roommate and their numerous college pranks before choking up in saying his final goodbye. Someone from the creative writing group wrote a poem to commemorate Hunter's life and, holding each other's hand at the lectern, Lynn and Lonnie composed a tearful farewell, which they delivered with dignified grace. No one in attendance had dry eyes.

Julie was disappointed that she could not spend more time with Alicia at the funeral home. She longed to know the young girl with whom she was confident Hunter had fallen in love. But the many visitors vying to console her warranted against it. The only real private moment was when Alicia asked if she could place the teddy bear Hunter had given her for Christmas in the casket with him. Julie and Russell graciously granted the appeal on the condition that she would come back soon to share with them the relationship she had with their son. Alicia cried. It was the very plea she was going to make of them. It was determined she would come as soon as she could arrange it.

In full view, Julie placed the fuzzy bear in the corner up by Hunter's head causing quite a few to ask about its significance. For that reason Alicia was introduced to a number of family and relatives as her son's girl friend. And for Julie, meeting her for the first time under such grave circumstances, created an instant special bond.

The Harrissons warmly welcomed the entire Collier family. They arrived the following day, stayed both nights and attended the Mass and luncheon. The two women shared tears as mothers; Brian was as shy as ever. But strangely, Harold, though very empathetic and prayerful, seemed very reticent, kept to himself in the back of the room continuously gazing at Hunter lying in the casket, and had a very difficult time looking directly at anyone else.

Intersections

He must have really taken to my son in such a short time, Julie thought as she observed him that first night standing alone, lost in thought.

But if the presence of loved ones tenderly eased her away from the precipice of despair to which Hunter's sudden death had propelled her, Julie was in no way prepared for the second dramatic shock three days later, after people had left and she caught up with her mail and read the accident report.

Oh, my God! She exclaimed with her hand on her forehead, definitively articulating each word with its own shocked emphasis. *Who could ever deny that there is someone with a plan for our lives!*

Yet, she procrastinated as to what to do or how to handle it after all these years.

The reconciliation continued each day. Russell hashed it out with Christine, admitting that he was using her as a midlife crutch, that he was upset at being a father again late in life. Said Hunter's death brought him to his senses. It was time to reaffirm his love and commitment to his wife and family. Voluntarily she left the firm and the area. Russell even spoke of returning to a smaller private practice, perhaps after their new baby was born and things were okay.

Julie has taken an extended leave, spending hours looking at pictures of Hunter in albums, touching over and over again the homemade valentines he had made in elementary school which she laid out on the coffee table, and speaking of her son's memory with Russell, the girls, friends, anyone who asked how she was doing.

And, of course, there were his clothes and belongings to disperse.

The placenta previa lessened, although the heavy strain of the past three weeks had taken a toll on the pregnancy. There was a second incident of unwarranted bleeding. Dr. Murasko gave strict orders to "do absolutely nothing, rest a lot and then rest some more", a formula quite unbearable when someone is in a period of sorrow. Julie obliged although it was particularly challenging to keep her mind on the present and look to the future.

"Said she'd be here tomorrow morning around 9:30," Russell said, hanging up the phone and turning to his wife. "I think I'll call off and stay home myself to greet her. I would love to know her a little better too." He tilted his head towards Julie. "If it's okay with you?"

"I'll just simply tell the office that I'm too distraught at the fact that the groundhog saw his shadow last week." Julie perched her lips and raised an eyebrow at his tongue in cheek reasoning.

Beckoning Russell to take her hand, Julie straightened her top and the two opened the front door.

"Hi."

Alicia stood there dressed in dark black slacks, her short winter jacket opened down the front revealing a modest orange blouse with a white ruffled collar, her hands hidden in each of the side pockets of the coat and a colorful tussle cap sitting atop her head. She looked as innocent and sweet as a school kid selling cookies for a fundraiser.

"Hello, Mr. and Mrs. Harrisson."

Harold Collier stood shielded behind her. That was a surprise.

Julie welcomed her with an affectionate hug and reached for her Dad's hand.

"Please come in. Welcome to our home." Russell hosted well. "May I take your coats?" The foursome settled around a newly lit fire in the living room.

"Can I get either of you something to drink? Coffee, juice, water?" Both guests declined the cordial offer by politely shaking their heads.

"Thank you for coming to the funeral with your whole family, Mr. Collier." Julie opened the dialogue.

"Harold ... please."

"Are you coming down from Garrison?"

"No, we drove from home yesterday. Stayed last night in town. Alicia did not return to school this semester." It was another surprise and the first of many disclosures to come.

Russell jumped in. "Oh, you would have been most welcomed to stay here."

"Thank-you, but we got in very late. We're going to Garrison when we leave here." Harold gestured towards his daughter sitting on the sofa with her hands folded between her knees. "Alicia wants to visit some of her friends. I promised we would." Smiling amiably, "It's been good for just the two of us to share this time together."

"The Mass was beautiful, Mrs. Harrisson."

"Yes, it was." Julie reached for her hand. "And how are you, honey? You were really fond of Hunter, weren't you?"

Alicia blinked her eyes a couple of quick times. "I was." Her voice quivered, "Mrs. Harrisson, I loved your son very much."

Julie moved over beside her and held her close for a few seconds. "Alicia, I'm so glad you came back to see us. But I *do* have to ask you something that's been bothering me ever since ... if you don't mind." She hesitated before continuing. "And please feel free to answer or not. I will understand."

Alicia flushed, waiting.

"Did you two have some type of quarrel or something? I mean we've been wondering why Hunter left to come home early?"

Julie's maternal intuition had told her during the past weeks that there was an explainable reason why he was on that bus that fateful day. "I wish he would have called to let us know he was coming home." Julie wandered in her thoughts. "But I guess it doesn't matter now."

"Well, that's not exactly what hap—"

"It's my fault!" Harold blurted out, which caused both Julie and Russell to suddenly turned to him in consternation.

"I asked your son to leave that morning ..." His voice trembled as he corrected himself. "No, I *insisted* he leave that morning. In fact I *personally* drove him to the terminal."

They were quiet; but the fire, as always, disregarded any uncomfortable silence with its minstrel show of sparks, snaps and crackles.

"I am responsible for your son's death." Harold sat rubbing his hands nervously. "It's because of me that your son was on that bus."

Julie and Russell, both with open mouths, had no words. Lost for any response, they felt very uncomfortable and bemused with the admission. Russell, in particular, looked down and fidgeted with his belt as he stood up and approached the fire to poke the logs.

"Daddy, please stop blaming yourself!" Alicia jumped to confront him face to face. "I know I screamed that at you that night, but you are NOT responsible for what happened. You didn't know there was going to be an accident. You were just being my Dad in the situation." She had his hands as she curved back to the sofa. "Please, Mr. and Mrs. Harrisson, help him stop blaming himself."

Russell joined Julie, putting his arm around her waist. "Of course, we don't blame anyone for Hunter's death. Bad things happen in life. That's all." Julie leaned forward. "But I still don't understand, Harold. *Why* were you so insistent that he leave your place early?"

Alicia sat back down beside them. Her expression had the answer. Instinctively, Julie knew the words before she said them.

"I'm pregnant."

"Oh."

Russell reacted pressing Julie's waist gently, his face falling but at the same time trying not to register any judgment.

"And I was livid. I was outraged and just wanted Hunter

Intersections

out of my house and my sight. I was furious at both of them and I immediately responded out of anger." Harold hesitated. "No. In all honesty, folks, I have to admit that your son – as I know now – was a fine gentleman." He glanced at his daughter. "I misjudged him completely. And after talking a lot more these last days with my daughter, I realize that he really and truly loved her."

Julie seemed resolved to have the ambiguity cleared up. "And that's why you …" Being the constant nurse, it struck her and she instantly reached for Alicia. "Are you okay, honey? Have you seen a doctor yet?"

Alicia nodded.

Russell moved closer to comfort also and looked up at Harold. "Can we help in anyway? We will gladly take our part as grand–"

Harold interrupted. "No, we're okay. I've gotten over it and her mother and I are prepared to take care of her and the baby until she gets on her own two feet."

"But we would be most willing to help … with anything we can … I mean, it will also be our grandchild." Russell spoke as Julie kept shaking her head gently. For a brief moment there was a joy in the thought that they might be grandparents.

Alicia and her Dad were silent.

"Alicia."

"I will Dad. Give me time."

Russell and Julie were perplexed again. They waited.

"Mr. and Mrs. Harrisson," she bit her lip, "I would give anything right now for this to be Hunter's baby." Pausing, "yes, we had a sexual relationship," she blushed, "but it was a good and loving thing … Hunter was so tender and gentle and…" Alicia began to cry.

"Shsssss, take your time, honey." Julie patted her hand. Harold stood with his hand on his daughter's shoulder.

Sniffing, "and as far as I'm concerned, Hunter will always be my child's father, but…" She played with the sapphire ring, nervously rotating it completely around her finger.

The fire roared. The phone rang. Everyone ignored it. They all sat quietly. Alicia cried softly, dabbing her eyes with a Kleenex.

"It's okay, Alicia." Harold said carefully massaging the back of her neck in support. "I think they should know. It'll be okay. They're good people and understanding parents."

Alicia took a breath. "But Hunter is not the father."

It had been said. Russell gripped his wife's waist as caringly as before.

Alicia took another breath, deeper this time, letting out a long sigh. "Last year when I was a sophomore, I got into a relationship with someone else. I was stupid because he was a total ass." With a determined voice, she vented her anger. "I'm sorry, but he was such a loser … and it was just sex, …nothing more, I promise you." Alicia put her head down. "I am so ashamed."

Harold rubbed her shoulders a little faster. Julie reassured her in a motherly tone that she was not the first one in life to experiment before "you think out the real consequences of your actions."

Alicia elaborated. "This kid and Hunter were the only two people I have ever slept with." She was embarrassed. "Please don't think I am a sleep around kind of person. It was just … just … a very stupid thing." The expressions on their faces guaranteed her they did not think ill of her. "I am ashamed to admit it." She pointed back at her Dad. "I have cried this out completely with my parents and it was tough. But they now know everything and are so supportive. Well …"

"Honey, do you need another Kleenex?"

"Yeah."

Julie started to rise. Russell motioned that she stay put and went to retrieve the tissue. Handing Alicia the flower-decorated box, he lovingly ran his hand down the back of her hair. Harold sat to support her with his arm.

Intersections

"The guy's name is Scott ... Scott Pincolior ... he graduated this past December. Lives in the Northwest." She spoke softly, confessing. "When I realized how gross he was, I wanted nothing to do with him ... realized it was stupid and I was wrong. At the same time I realized how much I was falling in love with Hunter." She looked up. "I am so sorry for all the hurt I have caused everyone. I was not even completely honest with Hunter. I never told him a thing." Pausing, "he never knew I slept with Scott the previous year. He always thought we were the first for each other." Looking down, "And I never told him what I'm about to tell you."

Julie squeezed her hand. The words about "not telling" jabbed at her gut. She listened with her eyes and her heart.

"Well ..." The heart of the story was the most agonizing. "The night I went back to school after Thanksgiving ... Hunter came back that same night and wanted me to go to a party with him ..."

She looked away, scrunching her nose and eyes. She turned the birthstone ring back and forth with intensity. "Oh, God, looking back, *how* I wish I had gone with him that night ... in Brian's dirty truck." She tossed her head and raised an eyebrow at the last words. That meant nothing to the three adults, not knowing how friends poked fun at Brian for his unkempt vehicle.

Harold held her tighter.

"Scott showed up and no one was around. He forced himself on me ..." Her head was bowed lower, "it's his child."

"Oh, honey, I am so sorry." Julie quickly moved to embrace her again. "That must have been so frightening for you. And you must have felt so alone all this time. Oh, I am so sorry."

"She told my wife and me everything the night you called with the devastating news about Hunter." Harold looked at his daughter. "She was yelling at me for making him go. I was angry that she was pregnant. And when I found out the entire story I was even more disappointed at her... at first ... until Nancy — err, my wife – reminded me that she's our daughter, right or wrong. Then I was mad at myself. She cautioned me that the problem isn't that we make mistakes – and we all do – but it's what we do with them that shows us the real test of a person."

"A wise woman, indeed," Julie replied.

Harold put his arms completely around Alicia. "I love my kids immensely and so I was even more enraged that somebody violated my daughter!" He stood for the next comments, pacing back and forth in front of the fireplace. "I contacted a lawyer in Oregon. We subpoenaed this Scott to have a paternity test. ... as hard as it was, I thought it best to know the truth." He stopped and frowned. "He *is* the biological father."

"My Dad wanted him charged and arrested for rape ... but as we talked – Mom and Dad and me — we decided not to go through a long court case."

"I did not want my daughter's good name dragged through the mud because of this idiot. You know how the heartless lawyers in these cases destroy the reputation of the girl ... it's always their fault! And since there had been consensual sex before, they would have said she asked for it!"

Russell and Julie listened with understanding and compassion. "But we did the next best thing. The lawyer had him sign a paper renouncing and relinquishing any and all rights to the baby forever and never to ever try to find him or her."

"And if he does ever come near them, he'll risk having 5 to 10 years in jail!" Harold interjected.

Alicia entreated them. "Mr. and Mrs. Harrisson, I want to have this baby as a sign of love, not violence. As far as I'm concerned, this is the child of the one I really loved ... your son." She stopped turning the ring and instead just held it, looking down at it.

Intersections

The fire was dying. Julie and Alicia cried and hugged at length. Russell and Harold supported their respective loved ones in silence.

Hunter's untimely death had brought out honesty in everyone.

The phone rang again. They ignored it as they spent the next couple of hours talking and sharing the bond that brought them together. Alicia and Harold both spoke of the way Hunter wanted to marry and take care of her and the baby. His son maturely accepting responsibility for his actions humbled Russell.

Julie rose. "Can we offer you lunch?"

Everyone was hungry. Emotions drain you of strength. "I think we would like that," Harold proffered.

"But first I need to get something."

Returning from upstairs, Julie handed Alicia the heart pendant. "This belongs to you. I believe you have the other half."

Closing it in her fist, and bowing her head, Alicia shut her eyes. "Thank-you."

"Now for that lunch." Julie reached out for her hand. "Come on, help me. Both being mothers-to-be, we have a lot to talk about."

Lynn and Lonnie bounced in the door from school wondering why Russell was home so early. They shared with them that Alicia had been there and that she was having a baby. In typical fashion, the twins bubbled with the notion that they were going to be aunts and couldn't wait to tell their friends.

"You coming to bed? It's been a long day. You must be exhausted."

Julie sat, feet propped up, a new fire prepared. A writing tablet and pen lay on the table in front of her. Beside them was the envelope with the accident report. "No, I'll be up later. I have a letter to write that should have been written a *very* long time ago."

"I understand." Russell whispered. "I love you."

"And I love you more than ever. I'll be up."

As he left, Russell turned. "You know, hon., its ironic."

"What is?"

"Well, the twists things take." He motioned towards the plump little bulge rising from her stomach, "I said it wasn't my child ... and it was. ... in all honestly I knew that it was... yet I was willing to deny it and disregard my responsibility." He complimented her. "I know you have been nothing but faithful to me all these years of marriage but in my selfish way I was willing for awhile to let people think it was not my problem. That it was yours."

He paused, looking down, "But Hunter thought it was his child ... and it wasn't ... but he was so ready to assume his responsibility... we really raised a good kid, didn't we?" He sighed. "You did a good job."

"*We* did a good job."

"Good night, honey."

It was the wee hours of the morning when Julie finally crawled in beside her husband.

Twenty

His smile was infectious, the light brown tuff of hair on his forehead as well as the distinguishing dimple near his boyish grin adding to the contagion of his congenial look. Greg surmised it was warm that day since Hunter wore faded cutoffs and sandals and a tie-dyed shirt. It was one of the four pictures Julie had sent with the letter, the picture leaning on the statue of Lady Knowledge and Science outside Phiny Hall. Brian, of course, was half hiding behind the statue, surreptitiously placing two fingers above Hunter's head as though he had sported horns. It was Julie's favorite picture from her son's college days. She duplicated it for Greg and he likewise chose it as his favorite of the four.

The others were taken at various times in the twenty-one years, one on a tricycle at two, a snapshot with the first fish he caught at the lake when he was around eleven, and his high school wallet graduation picture. The priest studied all four probably four zillion times since they came, but it was the one taken on the Garrison campus that Greg carried with him, tucked in the folds of the brown habit that crossed over his stomach. He chose to look at that one a lot more than the others.

"Ray, you have got to come up here tonight, immediately!" Corney remembered vividly the call from his best friend; he flew up the highway to the retreat center, risking a speeding ticket, thinking the worst. Instead he found Greg in his office, alone, the letter and pictures spread out on his desk in front of him, the most intriguing look on his face.

"Wow!"

Greg didn't respond. He simply toyed with the letter, sliding it from one side to the other with one hand, twirling the little bottle of white sand from the beach in his other, lost in his own world.

"You never knew?" Ray picked up the photo of Hunter on the tricycle, "I mean, did the possibility even cross your mind?"

Greg shook his head. "No. ... She disappeared from the base so fast. And no one would give me any information where she went. I thought that was strange and that's why I thought she hated me for ...maybe —" He looked like he was about to say something that he really didn't believe but considered that she might have, " ...taking advantage of her in *my* vulnerable state...I hated myself for losing control when I thought I should know better. After all, *I was* the priest, the chaplain, the one who knew right from wrong, and the one who advised everyone else how to act—"

"But you were also a young vibrant man, distraught, scared and wounded in a foreign land during a very unpopular war!"

"No excuse." Greg stood, pacing back and forth. "Come on, Ray. We've had this conversation almost word for word a hundred times but—"

"But you never knew she was carrying your child whenever--"

"You got that right!"

Greg kept pacing; Ray pondered how to ease the shock, how to convince him that what was so ... was so and that nothing could change the past.

"So, you've made your peace with the Lord, and with yourself and renewed your commitment to your vow of celibacy ... so—

"So?" Greg had his hands high in the air above his head, waving the picture in his hand like there was still something that should be or could be resolved.

"So thank God that you participated in the creation of new life, no matter how unorthodox the circumstances ... maybe it was meant to be ... including her never telling you and all."

Greg slumped back into his chair, almost touching the desk with his brow, propping his elbows perpendicular to his ears. "But *why* did she never tell me ... all these years?" The last three words were uttered like rapid gunfire in disbelief.

"Don't know. That's something you will have to ask her."

Looking up, "but yet it's crazy, Ray. I don't know if I want to know the answer ... don't want to know how much I may have messed up her life at that time ... and how much pain I caused—"

Corney was ready to hit him with a one-two humility punch and turn this thing positive.

"Greg!"

He fired his name like a parent trying to get the attention of a very distracted child who needed to be told something essential for its own safety.

Greg startled.

"Think of it!"

The commanding tone of voice had his attention.

"How unique you are with all of this! You not only gave this young man his natural life," Ray was brandishing the college picture he retrieved when Greg laid it down, "but the Lord gave you the privilege of ushering him into eternal life by letting *you* be the one to anoint him at the accident."

He paused long, for a dramatic effect.

"Coincidence? *I don't think so!*"

"I suppose you're right. As usual you have a way of putting things in a perspective that I don't always think about." Greg acquiesced but still had a lot of reflection to do before being fully at peace with the shocking news.

Ray sought to lighten things, flipping through all the pictures, going from one to the other and looping through them again, an odd smile on his face as though he were a little jealous of his brother. "Looks like you, okay."

"No he doesn't. He's better looking than I ever was at that age. If you remember, I was a skinny geek-looking nerd until I started to lift weights as a senior. Don't you remember the nickname I got in high school at the seminary?"

"Cu – cu – bun?"

"No, not that stupid thing. That was a silly made up thing on the spur of the moment one night at table when Ronnie Cassidy wanted something and couldn't get my attention. Everyone laughed and that also stuck for a while. No, I mean the affectionate one that even the teachers called me."

"What?"

"Peanuts."

"Oh, yeah, forgot about that one. Ha. I always like cu – cu – bun better!"

Greg reached for the college photograph again, "look how happy and fun loving he was. *This* is the one I want to imprint in my brain", tapping it with his finger three of four times in swift fashion, "... not the face I touched on that cold concrete highway."

Suddenly, the smile morphed a little into a slight frown. "But there is still a punishment here ... ironically ..."

"Yeah?"

"I really can't share the joy nor the sadness with just

anyone. With the way the Church hides scandal and all—"

"But Greg, that was so long ago ... it may not scandalize the faithful, as they say, as much as you think today ... if they knew and understood the *whole* story."

"Maybe, but it's best that only you and I know. Okay?"

"Whatever you say."

The two continued the conversation, walking for some time on the path up in the back near the gardens despite the brisk cold February air. Greg felt warmhearted inside; reliving what he thought was the *whole* story from those summer months so long ago.

He stopped in his tracks. "Ray! I had a son!"

"Yes you did."

"You know he was good at telling a joke."

"Huh?"

"That's how Julie described him ... as much as she could in just a few pages." Greg started to stroll slowly. "But there's so much more I want to know. She said he played the guitar. Was he good at it? Did he play anything else? What did he like the most to do? What did he want to do with his life?" He asked a rhetorical question with almost every step. "Simple things like: did he like to watch professional football as much as I do? And serious ones like: did he get diabetes from me? Where was he going or coming from that day?"

"Are you going to call her, get back in touch with her?"

"I don't know. I just don't know what to do."

Perhaps he was wrong. Perhaps it was just a romantic fiction of his imagination all these years. Maybe in reality he had caused a young, beautiful woman a lot of heartache and pain instead.

They meandered until the chill got too much and they headed inside to join the fraternity of the other brothers.

Greg propped up his elbows on the vestment drawers, his fists supporting his chin, the favorite picture once more lying before him on the cabinet counter. Someone entered; he swiftly tucked the print into the liturgical book.

"I have everything out for you, Father. Do you need anything else?" It was Brother Martin, the retreat house sacristan. "And I cut some yellow dahlias from the garden for the altar."

"Ahhh, thanks, Martin. I appreciate it and you don't have to come back. I know it's your day off. I'll put everything away." He remembered something else. "By the way, please ask Mark if the guest house is clean and available in case anyone in this group wants to stay."

"I already did. He assured me he completely cleaned it after Fr. Tim's relatives used it last month for the July 4th holiday. And nobody has used it since then. So it should be okay."

Greg snuck another peek at Hunter's picture. He was a bundle of nerves and couldn't recall ever being this anxious about anything in his life, not at ordination, not when he celebrated his parents' funerals or even when he landed in Da Nang.

They did talk by phone, two days after he received the letter, with Ray still challenging him to muster the courage. But Julie beat him to the punch. She called to follow up that he received it. He almost made himself unavailable suffering an intense approach-avoidance feeling. But finally he picked up the phone, stammering a few platitudes, niceties, and enduring a fair amount of silence on the line.

And there were other conversations, mostly friendly and affable; mostly updating the years since they last saw each other. Julie told him where she went in Germany, about Russell and the twins, and moving to Mentor. Greg relayed his traveling with the mission band of preachers for almost eight years when he returned from Vietnam, the parish work he did, and lastly being assigned as the director of Alverno.

In that first stilted call, Julie thanked him greatly for anointing Hunter and for just being at the accident. He accepted her appreciation silently. When they talked again, she filled in more details about Hunter's life and personality, how proud she was of him, what a good person he had developed into, how much she missed him. Greg heard her softy crying with the last words.

They weren't many, a total of three calls including the last one asking and making arrangements for today. But in all of the phone exchanges, both skirted unanswered questions and unsaid thoughts. After all, they were not two young people in love anymore; they were adults who had lived separate lives with no contact all these years. Greg honestly did not know how to approach what he really wanted to know.

"Fr. Greg."

Still leaning over the high table, Greg experienced a vast flood of emotion with that soft voice behind him at the door. It was as though in an instance, a time machine whisked him back to the first time he heard that innocent, melodious inflection on China Beach.

Smarting from the explosion of the booby-trapped music box when Duane had saved him from being killed, depressed over the whole notion of war and people hating each other, and feeling tremendously lonely at the moment, he walked the beach just as the dusk was losing the battle and the darker shades of a quarter moonlit night were conquering. He was praying and complaining, screaming out loud at the same time, in the same breath to God. Greg was angry, pounding his fist one into the other as he walked in the sand, releasing the fierce tensions in his soul and searching for some bit of sanity in this hellish situation.

"Hey, soldier, you okay?"

The utterance startled him. He thought he was completely alone and did not see her. But she sat back from the water up against the rocks, hidden in the black shadows, also alone.

"I'm sorry. I didn't think anyone was out here. I didn't—"

"Want anyone to hear you bitching and moaning?"

Greg was embarrassed. "Yeah, I guess that's what I was doing. Sorry."

"Don't be sorry! You have every right to be angry at all the crap in this hellhole. I am!" She walked into the dim moonlight and realized who the stroller was. "Oh, I'm sorry, Father. Talking like that and all."

The young woman was so cute in her shorts and halter-top, bare feet, her hair blowing freely on the back of her neck. At the moment, titles and priesthood and all the glory he thought this stint as a chaplain would be, was irrelevant.

"Greg."

"Okay ... Greg."

She walked closer as he stopped in his tracks, his own feet in the white bubbles just at the surf's edge. He recognized her as Julie Rainer, one of the prettiest nurses in the medical tent tending to him and the others. In a way he was stunned by her negativity since everyone said she was the most pleasant of all. But ever the most optimistic person in the world had to be confounded by the fog of war.

"How's the leg?"

"Okay."

But it wasn't. It was throbbing; the pain pills were totally ineffective. He hid the limp.

"You were pretty ripped up by the bomb's blast when Duane carried you in. Both of you were in bad shape."

"Yeah, I know."

"You're were trembling all over, disoriented and throwing up with fright."

Greg looked down in mortification. "Yeah I guess I was."

"You still scared?" She was direct.

Greg dropped all pretence of being *'the priest'*, the strong one, and the calm one who could console and explain things. He confessed meekly.

Intersections

"Yes, I am."

Those three words, finally broken loose from his heart to the ears of a beautiful tender-loving woman, were just what he needed to dispel the hideous fear shredding his gut. They both meandered to sit by the dune together, listening to the waves and wound up talking for a couple of hours about all kinds of things — the beach, the war, how afraid she was too, why she volunteered as a nurse to come here, why he was a priest, how glorious and noble he thought it would be to volunteer as a chaplain, how naive he was about people wanting to kill each other.

They walked and talked again the next night, and the next and the next, absolutely comfortable in each other's presence, open to sharing the inner recesses of their hearts to one another.

Now she stood in the doorway of the sacristy watching him with his back to her. He had not changed much as he hunched over, a little heavier but not much, still the imposing presence, yet exuding compassion. Julie was flooded with guilt from keeping the knowledge of Hunter from him all these years. For a brief moment, she regretted being there, wanted to bolt out of there but then she came to her senses. The past was the past. Regretting would not change it. There was nothing she could do about it now but try to be thankful for the few years she had with Hunter and the fact that Greg did get to touch him. Finally, *this* was the right thing to do, the right time and the right place.

"Hi."

The simply sound of her voice in the doorway sparked it all rushing back, the night they kissed for the first time and how flustered he was yet how enthralled; the night she shared the story of a young private, who left behind a wife and a 15 month old daughter that he never saw, dying in her arms that day and cried while Greg held her; the feeling of falling in love with her in such a short time and allowing passion to rule his mind and body. It all came back in a flash.

Greg turned. Julie was as radiant as ever. It was just as he remembered her, but wiser looking and perhaps a little tested. Greg's impulse was to sweep her up and run back into that romantic dream and never let go this time. Her voice on the phone was one thing these past months, but being here in person, his knees quivered. Facing her, his heart did a back flip like an infatuated teenager.

"Hi."
"How are you?"
"Fine."
"Glad you could come."
"Thank you for having us and agreeing to do this."

At first Julie hesitated to move. It was the first time she actually saw Greg in his simple Franciscan habit. In Vietnam it was military fatigues, shorts on the beach or a hospital gown. She walked over slowly and with open palms took both of Greg hands in hers. "I am so sorry. I owe you an enormous apology."

He said nothing. Her touch ran through him creating every good emotion possible. It was as though the one time in his life that he truly experienced real human love as a man had happened only five seconds ago. Could he freeze-frame this feeling forever?

"You had every right to know ... all these years. I was so wrong not to tell you." Julie looked up into his eyes. Greg almost felt they were miles away from Alverno, again on the sand. "You don't know how many times I wanted to call ... write ... tell you ... and couldn't get to that point." She lowered her head. "I guess once I kept if from you, it became easier with each day and year."

Spontaneously the question tumbled out, the question struggling inside since Vietnam and totally revived with the letter. "Why did you leave so fast? And not let me know anything ... or let anyone else tell me anything?"

Julie looked up again. "Because I *had* fallen in love with you."

The words seared as though they shot through her hands directly to his heart. Again that unbelievable, thrilling feeling! He was speechless; the inquiring frown on his face intensified.

"You were everything I wanted in someone ... I really did love you ... in such a short time. I asked to be transferred and you not be told." She paused. "And it was shortly afterwards in Germany when I found out that I was carrying your baby," Julie paused longer, "that I determined that I wasn't going to tell you because I *did* love you."

The words of love were spine tingling, but the answer seemed very contradictory.

"I know that sounds very strange and –"

Greg squinted his eyes, squeezed her hands tighter and said. "But I don't understand. I mean if you loved me ... and I fell in love with you, then why—"

Julie let go and stepped back a little.

"I constantly heard so many of the guys talk about how you helped them ... as a priest. I knew the way you talked you were happy as a priest and—"

"And?"

"And I didn't want to mess up your life ... being what you wanted to be ... a priest ... and it just couldn't be ... you, me, a child ... I was afraid you would leave the priesthood for me."

Her explanation was so loving and gentle. "I was convinced that I had led you on... and I didn't think you would be happy if you left your vocation ... for me ... that so many people that I'm sure you have helped over all these years would have been denied that help." Julie repeated. "I decided to just get out of your life ... go ... I knew you would survive and go on being a good and caring priest ..."

She reached for both hands again. "But I was wrong to keep you from knowing that Hunter was your son. You had a right to know and I apologize."

Greg was blown away. He stared.

"And when I read that it was *you* at the accident ... *you* that anointed him, I was totally ashamed at my not telling. I knew it was God's way of reminding me that I was wrong ... all these years!" She glanced down. "And I couldn't really say it in the letter or on the phone ... I had to say this in person." Julie opened her hands in petition, her eyes locked on his. "Can you ever forgive me?"

Slowly Greg pulled the photograph from the ritual book lying there. "He was a great kid, wasn't he?"

The two held the picture together.

"The best. Just like you. Caring, gentle, fun-loving. Always interested in others." Greg saw tears as Julie moved her finger back and forth on the picture.

"Would it be inappropriate ... to ask if I could hug you?"

"I would like that."

Two adults with totally separate stories bridged the past with one more embrace that signaled forgiveness and the closing of an unfinished chapter in both of their lives.

Greg let her go arms length. "I am so thankful our paths crossed in life. I do think I've been a better person for knowing you."

They hugged again.

The past was resolved.

"Russell knew, of course, all these years. Do your girls know?"

"No. And I made another gigantic mistake. I never told Hunter."

Greg's continence dropped.

"Russell kept admonishing me, and my conscience kept telling me that I should when he was old enough to understand ... and recently Elena prodded me ... and I came so close when Hunter and I were alone together this past Christmas—"

"Elena Meltrant? You kept in touch all these years?"

Intersections

"Actually, no. We just renewed out friendship last November when she was in Cleveland giving a talk and looked me up. She's a renowned endocrinologist in London."

"Really?"

"Yeah, and it was no coincidence, I feel. She has been *major* in my life these last months, helping me over a rough patch with Russell not accepting the late pregnancy at first, through Hunter's death and the birth when things got a little harrowing." Julie motioned to the chapel. "She's here with us."

Greg heard Ray in his mind: *Coincidence? I don't think so!*

"And now, I can't make up for that mistake ... he's not here for me to tell—"
She put her face in her hands.

Greg embraced her again warmly. "You'll see him again, someday." It was the priest in him talking ... to his one true love. "I promise."

Silence.

"You okay?"

Julie nodded.

"Hey, we better not keep everyone waiting. We have a couple of babies to baptize." She smiled as she watched him don the white vestment and place the long stole over his neck, with the words *baptized with water ... bathed in light,* embroidered down each side.

Russell's brother stood beside him as the godfather, Julie held the baby and Elena at her side as the godmother. Lynn and Lonnie found strategic places on either side to each take a role of pictures of the event with their instant cameras.

The Colliers stood together with Brian Parks and Marcy from Garrison as sponsors for the other infant.

Fr. Greg addressed the people before him. "Is it your intention that these children be baptized in the faith that we profess?"

211

Jim Caldwell

Both mothers proudly professed. "Yes."

Fr. Greg spoke to Julie's group on the left. "By what name are we to call this child?"

"Brandon Paul."

The little one squiggled his eyes and suckled his tiny lips at the sound of his name

With an overwhelming joy in his heart, the priest turned to the family on the right, addressing in particular the beaming young woman. "By what name are we to call this child?"

His heart leapt with her answer.

"Hunter Joseph."

Printed in the United States
67025LVS00001B/61-99